WHEN WE'RE LEAST EXPECT...

For my friend and
Colleague Stoned,

Thank you for
your encouraging
comments!

Dee Fitzwilliam

February 2015

WHEN WE'RE LEAST EXPECTING IT

Dee Fitzwilliam

ROMAN *Books*
www.roman-books.co.uk

Copyright © 2014 Dee Fitzwilliam

ISBN 978-93-80905-67-9

Typeset in Dante MT Std

First published in 2014

1 3 5 7 9 8 6 4 2

British Library Cataloguing in Publication Data.
A catalogue record for this book is available from the British Library.

Publisher: Suman Chakraborty

ROMAN Books
26 York Street, London W1U 6PZ, United Kingdom
Suite 49, Park Plaza, South Block, Ground Floor, 71, Park Street, Kolkata 700016, WB, India
2nd Floor, 38/3, Andul Road, Howrah 711109, WB, India
www.roman-books.co.uk | www.romanbooks.co.in

Printed and bound in India by
Repro India Ltd.

For Frédérique, who left us too soon.
Repose en paix, chérie.

And to the cherished memory of MD—always in mind.

ONE

Istanbul: July 1994

'*Merhaba canim! Istanbul'da hoş geldiniz!*' Mehmet stood just inside the automatic doors to the airport's main exit. Behind him, through the glass, taxi drivers stood about, leaning on one another's cars; smoking; each twirling beads idly in one hand as they chatted; greeting the arrival of each driver known to them; they laughed; spat.

Barbara acknowledged Mehmet's welcome with the expected response, '*Hoş bulduk*', meaning 'a welcome is found.' She was surprised to see Mehmet looking exactly as he had twelve months earlier—just as beautiful—almost outrageously good-looking. In the intervening months since their—what—*relationship?* started—well, since she had met him anyway, she'd had photos and letters, but somehow, to see him before her now, holding a small bunch of flowers, was strange—as if he had ceased to exist 'in reality' until this moment.

'Flowers for me? You are sweet.' She 'parked' her small wheelie case and stood on tiptoe to kiss his cheek. 'I'm gasping for a coffee—is there anywhere open here? Sure isn't that the trouble with these cheap flights—arriving in the middle of the night?'

'I have a taxi right here—my cousin, Atila, he drives. He will take us to hotel. There we can have a drink. I get you the best room—of course!'

Mehmet was managing a small, old-style hotel in the Sultan Ahmet district of Istanbul, right underneath the mosque itself. It was 'no problem', he had said in his letter, to book out the roof-terrace room for Barbara for the week. Now in the cab, swinging along around the ring road, past the old walls of Istanbul, where, the guidebooks said, there could still be seen evidence of the fish ponds used by monasteries—but which Barbara had never found, despite several trips in search of them.

Suddenly, Mehmet and Atila's conversation, in Turkish, grew louder and more animated.

'What's wrong?' Barbara asked.

'Wrong? There is nothing—what do you mean?'

'Why are you shouting? What are you arguing about?'

'He is asking about my family, that is all. And I'm telling him about my mother and sister, and asking about my aunt. No argument.'

Barbara had a momentary feeling of 'disconnection', of not understanding what was going on, and felt far from home, far from 'the known', which made her both anxious and excited.

Atila's taxi pulled up outside The Hotel Meydan. They said goodbye and he drove away—waving his arm out of the window, promising to come back one evening when he didn't have to work, to spend some time with them.

Four flights of winding stairs—no lift. Mehmet had a small, round-faced boy take Barbara's case up to the roof-terrace room, while they went into the breakfast room—all laid up ready for next morning—and he busied himself at the bar, making coffee.

'It's amazing to be here again,' she said. 'And to be here with you'.

'Of course it is—you are my amazing woman.' When he said things like this, so very seriously, it was hard not to laugh, but she knew not to—she just knew he might be hurt if she made light of his overly-romantic turns of phrase.

'Are there many people staying here at the moment?'

'Some. Most come tomorrow. Saturday. English women are here—two of them. Old . . . no, I mean not old, but more than you. They share a room.'

Barbara lit a cigarette, sat back in her chair and studied the room. All the familiar things: the *Efes* beer adverts and bar towels, the tiny tea glasses on the shelves, the faded travel posters of Pamukkale and Nemrut Dag. The round-faced boy appeared, smiling shyly, and spoke to Mehmet in Turkish.

'This is Osman—he says you are pretty woman.'

'Thank you—he's a charmer, isn't he? How old is he?'

'He is seventeen but he knows people think he is younger. He has hard time finding girlfriend—they all want to be a mother with him!'

'They want to "mother" him, you mean'

'That's what I said.'

'No, what you said was . . . oh don't worry, it's too late to explain—it's nearly three am, no wonder I feel tired.'

'Here, I made you cappuccino—it will make you awake again.'

'I wouldn't count on it, but thanks, that looks great.'

As she spooned the foamy froth into her mouth, slowly, Mehmet sat opposite her, lit a cigarette, and stared at her. He was about to speak when Osman called to him. He replied in his own language.

'He is going now—he says "goodnight", he will come tomorrow.'

'*Iyi geceler*, Osman, see you tomorrow. Thanks for taking my bag.'

'You do not have to thank him, he works for me.'

'It is polite to thank people, *canim*, and I like to thank people who help me.'

'Is the coffee waking you?'

'It's just nice to drink it—I'm very tired though. I think I should go to bed soon.'

'Do you want me to be with you tonight?'

'I feel awkward, now. All the things we've said in letters about when we would be together, and now we are . . . I don't know. It's just that . . .'

'It is all right—I want to talk to you about everything, first, I mean, before . . . tomorrow we can talk, and tonight I have my room over there.' He indicated a door next to the reception area.

'That's probably best,' she said.

'*Haydi*—come on then, I'll show you the room.'

They climbed the winding stairs, passing doors off here and there to other floors, rooms, bathrooms, passing little alcoves with plastic vases of plastic flowers in them.

'My flowers!' Barbara said, suddenly, seeing these. 'I left the flowers you gave me in the taxi! I'm so sorry.'

'It doesn't matter—I will get you some more. Here we are.'

They stepped out of the stairwell onto the roof—the rooftops and especially the staggeringly beautiful domes of Sultan Ahmet—The Blue Mosque—were illuminated against an indigo sky—it took Barbara's breath away.

'It's so . . . the view . . . wonderful . . . magical.'

Through double doors from the terrace, a smallish double bed still managed to fill most of the room. A wash basin next to the bed. A tiny shower room with toilet and a small alcove containing a one-ring stove and battered fridge.

'Is it OK, the room?' Mehmet asked her.

'It's just fine,' she said. '*And,*' she thought, '*as he's insisted that I don't pay for it, it's actually far better than "just fine"!*'

'Do you mind if I just smoke one cigarette out there while you put your things away?'

'No—well, I'm not going to unpack much now—too late. But I'll get my washing things out and I'll come and join you outside for a last ciggie. I still can't believe that view.'

Barbara unzipped her case and removed her washbag and her West African *boubou*, a cotton kaftan-like garment that she favoured instead of a dressing gown. It was one of many she'd brought back from Senegal on a trip for the development agency she worked for. '*So many memories and souvenirs,*' she thought, '*even in my clothes!*' She moved to the basin, ran the tap and splashed cold water on her face, then dried herself on the thin towel; decided to clean her teeth— '*Always makes one feel better*'.

Feeling refreshed, she went outside.

'*Tamam*—OK?' Mehmet was half-sitting, half-leaning against the parapet wall of the terrace.

'Yes, it's fine . . . great. Listen—the birds are waking up.'

Birdsong was starting, here and there, among the trees scattered along the dusty streets, signalling the coming dawn. Barbara stood in front of Mehmet, he shuffled up onto the wall and spread his legs wide, wrapping them around her.

'There—I catch you!' he laughed.

She looked up at him and as she did so, he wrapped his arms around her as well, embracing her in a passionate kiss.

Feelings that she had not experienced for very long time stirred Barbara. She returned his kiss enthusiastically. A thousand thoughts racing through her head—including the thought that she *did* want him to share her bed that night—or wanted simply to rip off their clothes there and then on the terrace and give in to their passion.

But Mehmet stopped kissing her—moved her away from him and slid down from the wall.

'It's late,' he said, 'and you must sleep. I will come in the morning— well, later on—it is already morning. Goodnight, *canim.*'

And with that, he strode across the terrace and disappeared down the stairs.

TWO

Barbara had met Mehmet while travelling with her husband, Gareth, an academic librarian, one year earlier, while they were waiting for a *dolmuş* taxi in a tiny place on the west coast of Turkey. Mehmet had started chatting in English to them both on the journey, and they swapped addresses when the *dolmuş* rolled into their destination. They had returned home to Oxford with many such addresses—but something had happened between Barbara and Mehmet. She was convinced that there had been 'something' sparking between them, but it was not until she received the first letter from him that she found herself proved right.

His letter was full of questions—and assertions—about her marriage. Barbara almost resented this—it felt like a betrayal—but then she realised that what irked her most was that her feelings could be so easily 'read' by this good-looking stranger. She'd hoped she was a better actor than that. But he'd met them, and worked it all out, in just a few kilometres' journey in a battered minibus. 'How long is it you are sad?' he'd written. And: 'You are brother and sister relationship, not like real marriage?'

And so it began. They exchanged letters, and a few phone calls. There seemed safety and anonymity in the distance between them, which caused Barbara to tell Mehmet things that were kept from even close friends at home.

Gareth had been diagnosed with kidney disease within weeks of their marriage. He'd never been particularly easy to live with, almost sociopathic, and as his health worsened, Barbara fell into the role of carer—protecting him from having to deal with the day-to-day running of their life together. They had not had sex for about a year, at the time they travelled to Turkey; and there had been none since, either. Gareth had been due to start dialysis in the September of that year, and so they decided to take the holiday as it might be his last chance to travel abroad for a while—if ever. They had started off in Istanbul, for a week, and then travelled across to the Asian side and made their way around a great loop, taking in Canakkale, Ephesus, Bergama, Troy, Ayvalik, Pammukkale, all the way across to Afyon, and then back up to Istanbul for a final two days.

Barbara convinced herself that their relationship was not that unusual. She told herself that her beloved home town of Oxford was full of couples who lived 'separate lives'; lived in two separate houses, even, and no-one thought of them as any 'less married' than other couples. But deep down, she knew that these people were by-and-large wealthy academic types, with the luxury of owning two properties in which to lead their separate, eccentric lives. And it would be OK, she thought, if she *could* lead a separate life—as it was, all she had in common with these other couples was that she didn't have sex with her husband any more. The difference was that she didn't have sex at all, and tyrannised by Gareth's bad moods, just got on with doing whatever he wanted to do in the evenings and at weekends. This was reading, usually, or watching French and Italian 'Art House' films on video. 'Watching films' sounds OK, but with Gareth, it was 'forbidden' to speak during the film, or to pause it to make coffee—she'd make a flask up before the start. She dreaded having to go for a pee in the middle of a film—as he'd get stroppy if she asked to pause the film.

Sometimes Gareth would choose a book to read aloud to her—which she did enjoy—but it was always *his* choice, everything always on *his* terms, and so life went on. Later, she would realise that at the time it had never occurred to her that there could be anything better, anything different, for her.

Her job, at least, gave her the chance to travel. She worked as a researcher for an international development agency and went on trips to visit projects—mainly in West Africa and Eastern Europe—fairly regularly. She'd become used to travelling alone, and enjoyed it. She'd had numerous 'adventures' on her travels, incidents which made her wonder, constantly, how it was that she had never been mugged, raped, or murdered! She kept journals on her travels, and she had read excerpts of the first ones to her late mother, who would widen her eyes and say 'No! Don't tell me any more, I'll worry so about you on your next trip . . . what happened next?'

One of her mother's favourite stories had been the one about Barbara returning to her hotel on Goree Island, off Dakar, the capital of Senegal, late at night. She'd got the midnight ferry, having spent the evening at a live concert of wonderful West African music in the city's 'Medina' district. Once on board, she realised that she was the only woman on the boat, and felt slightly nervous about having to walk from the beach-jetty to her hotel once the boat docked. She did a quick 'recce' of the other passengers. There were two white men amongst them, one youngish and dressed in a traditional kaftan-like *boubou* (as, indeed, was she); the other an elderly gent, who looked like a writer or artist, with his floppy, felt hat and bow tie. She decided that once they arrived she would ask to walk to the hotel with one of them for safety.

Twenty minutes later, everyone began to stand up and form a queue to disembark. Barbara approached the younger man: *'Excusez-moi, monsieur . . .'*

The man took one look at her and waved her away, saying *'Non! Non!'*

Discouraged and slightly alarmed by his reaction, Barbara was then caught up in the melee as the boat unloaded its passengers and supplies, and found herself on the jetty, where she spotted the elderly man, who was sitting on an enormous suitcase, so she approached him.

At this point, Barbara realised a universal truth: if you have only a basic grasp of a foreign language, in this case, French, what little you know will abandon you in a crisis. What she *meant* to say was simply 'Would you mind if I walked with you to the hotel for safety as it is late and dark?' What she *actually* said to the man, in French, went something like: 'Excuse me, sir, but I wondered . . . could you come with me to my hotel . . . it is only over there, but the night, you know it is dark and the stars . . . and I wondered . . . could we be together . . . um . . .'

At which, the elderly man placed a hand on Barbara's arm and replied that he was sorry, but his friend was coming to meet him but he thanked her for asking him! As there was only one hotel on the island, Barbara soon realised that it was likely that he would be going there anyway, and sure enough, as she started to walk away from the jetty, another elderly white man arrived and greeted his friend. A young black man hefted the huge case onto a sack trolley, and they all started walking not far behind Barbara, in the same direction. Later, in bed, writing up the day's events in her journal, Barbara couldn't stop laughing at what the poor old gent must have thought of her. The first man on the boat obviously thought she was a hooker, and the second one thought she was propositioning him as well!

Next morning, when Barbara went down to the terrace for breakfast, she saw the two elderly men sitting at one of the tables. As she descended the steps, she saw the one from the boat lean forward and say to his friend: '*C'est elle, là!*'—'That's her, there!' He'd obviously told his friend about her and what she'd said to him the night before. Barbara smiled—she hoped she'd made an old man happy, at least!

Yes, her job and travelling gave Barbara a wealth of stories and anecdotes, and more importantly, she believed, a sense of perspective. And the ability to appreciate how lucky she was to be an educated, middle-class European woman, with the freedom that went with it.

THREE

After Mehmet left, Barbara went into her room and laid on the bed. She stared at the ceiling, trying to arrange her thoughts and feelings, but sleep overtook her. She was woken only a short time later, with the ear-splittingly loud *ezan*—the call to prayer—from the many-megaphoned domes of Sultan Ahmet. She was freezing cold, and it took a few seconds for her to 'come- to' in the strange surroundings. All around, other mosques started up their own *ezans*, and suddenly it was morning. Street sounds: cars, delivery vans; people moving around—going about their business. Somewhere a radio played Turkish pop music of the type Barbara remembered from interminable bus journeys the year before.

Out on the terrace, she heard a chair scraped back, and the 'chink' of glass and cutlery. She slipped off the bed and moved the thin material covering the doors a fraction to peer out. There was Osman, the young man from the night before, laying breakfast things on the table from a large tray. As she watched, Mehmet appeared from the stairs, and they started speaking in rapid Turkish.

Another man appeared, a little older than Mehmet, who was twenty-three. They greeted one another, and then the two older men drew aside, leaving Osman to his work. The stranger jerked his head towards her room, and from this, and the way he seemed to be emphasising his words with definite movements of his hands, Barbara sensed they were talking about her. They both looked towards where she was standing, and she quickly stepped back.

She decided to shower quickly and go out to greet both the day and whatever it might bring.

'Ah yes,' she thought as she stepped into the shower room, '*Turkish plumbing!*' The pipework groaned as she turned the lever. Cold water spat from the shower head, together with a lot of air, and eventually, after a considerable amount of belching and knocking from said plumbing, she was able to wash under a vaguely warm, and positively reluctant sprinkling of water.

She dried herself on her own, large, soft, bath towel, brought from home—she'd experienced too many of the tiny, thin things that passed as towels in the cheaper hotels and guest houses of the world. Mehmet was knocking at the door—'Barbara—are you awake?' he called.

'Just a minute—I'll be right there,' she replied, wondering why she felt exposed, embarrassed almost. She went to the door and opened it a little, holding the towel around her 'I won't be a minute, I'm just getting dressed.' The sun was now up properly, and the light was dazzling.

'Did you sleep OK?' he asked.

'I didn't sleep very long, but I feel better after my shower. You OK?' She noticed that Mehmet was now alone on the terrace.

'Yes, fine. Come on, I have breakfast up here for you.'

Barbara pulled on her jeans and put on one of her loose-fitting long-sleeved tee-shirts. She then put on a headscarf 'pirate-style', with fringes falling down to the right side of her neck and collarbone. '*Not bad, considering the lack of sleep,*' she thought as she quickly applied a touch of mascara. '*And not bad for an old 'un, as my ma used to say!*' She was thirty-two years old, but with her child-like fascination for life, and sense of fun, often would pass for a good five years younger. She went outside.

On the table there were small dishes of olives, cubes of white cheese, sliced cucumber; hard-boiled eggs; a rack of toast; a coffee pot and a small mug. There was a small white jug in the centre, with flowers in it—some of them looking rather sad, rather crushed and wilted.

'Oh, more flowers for me.'

'No, they are your flowers—same flowers,' he said.'

'What do you mean, "same flowers"?'

'Atila brought them, this morning, early—he found them and when he is going home he brings them for you.'

'What? He works all night driving his taxi and then comes here just to bring them back to me?'

'Yes, he is very nice friend, very kind person.'

'You're telling me!'

'Come—have your breakfast, I'll be back soon—I have to see the other guests downstairs.'

Barbara lingered over her breakfast. The sun was hot but the breeze and the parasol over the table made it possible for her to enjoy it, she was definitely not a 'sun worshipper'. Her favourite time of year was winter, she always said, and she loved snow, log-fires, roast Sunday dinners and all that went with that season. But she also loved swimming in the sea, for which two things were necessary, in her opinion: it had to be on a summer's day and it had to be in a hot country. The bracing British seaside was not for her!

It was nearly an hour later and Mehmet had not returned. She had finished her breakfast and smoked a cigarette with a second, lukewarm, mug of coffee. She went to her room, cleaned her teeth, picked up her bag and went downstairs.

Mehmet was standing behind the Reception desk, facing two middle-aged women who, just by looking at them, Barbara knew to be English. The larger woman looked up when Barbara appeared, and they both gave a start of recognition.

'Hello my dear, what are you doing here? How lovely to see you. Are you with Gareth?'

It was the wife of one of 'The Profs', as Gareth called the tutors at the university anthropology faculty where he worked. Henry Morbesson was an incredibly ancient man, an expert on the Marsh Arabs of Iraq. Indeed, he and his wife (whose name Barbara couldn't remember at all), were one of those 'academic couples' with separate lives she'd been thinking about recently in relation to her own marriage. And here was the wife, standing before her with a slightly younger and slimmer woman, and asking about Gareth.

'Oh—er . . . yes! I mean, no, I'm on holiday but Gareth's not able to travel at the moment—his dialysis, you know. Er, I'm so sorry, but I can't remember your first name.'

'That's all right, dear, it's Rosalind, and this is my companion, Margaret Jennings.'

Barbara shook hands with Margaret, whose long, thin, fingers she felt feared she would crush as she did so. Margaret was pale and fragile, perfectly suited to the cotton print dress she wore.

Barbara remembered with a smile something her friend Jeremy had once said: 'Hmm . . . Laura Ashley—sexy it ain't'.

'Pleased to meet you,' Margaret was saying, 'Are you from Oxford too?'

'Yes, Rosalind's husband and mine work together. How long have you been here?'

'We've been here a fortnight and next week we're off to Ankara to see some friends of Rosalind's there. We like this hotel, it's so small and friendly isn't it?'

Before Barbara could answer, Rosalind broke in—'Well, we were just going to the Post Office to send off some postcards, shall we see you later?' She started to usher Margaret towards the door.

'Perhaps we can meet up for tea this afternoon? How long are you here for?' said Margaret over her shoulder.

'I only arrived last night—I'm here for a week. Yes, tea would be nice—but I'm not sure what I'm doing . . .' Barbara glanced at Mehmet, and then realised that such a glance, if seen by the two women, might give away her relationship with him.

'OK,' Rosalind's booming voice continued, 'We'll be over in the tea shop gardens by the museum at about three o'clock—come along if you feel like it. Do you know where I mean?'

'Oh yes, I spent quite a lot of time there last year, when I was here—with Gareth. Might see you later, then.'

When they'd gone, Barbara turned to Mehmet. 'Oh Christ! Of all the people to be staying here!'

19

'You know these women? They are the ones I told you about. We think they are, you know, gay women—lovers!'

'I really don't know—Rosalind and her husband each have a large house of their own—he's very old now. I guess it's possible, although they could just be friends who travel together.'

Mehmet, who had been joined by Osman, laughed and said: 'You just accept it and think about it like that? It is normal for you to know these gay women?'

Osman and he were like a couple of giggling children as Mehmet spoke to him in Turkish, telling him what had just happened.

'Oh sure, I'm not bothered by it at all—if people find happiness in being with another person, who cares who the other person is? It's just really weird that they should be here—when I'm here too.'

'You think she will say something to Gareth when you are all back home?'

'What could she say? He knows I'm here, and knows I'm coming to see you. So what's to say? Anyway, why should they think anything other than I'm on holiday here on my own—that's the situation, isn't it?'

Mehmet gave her a look that said 'Yeah, right', and asked Osman to take over at the Reception Desk.

'Go into the lounge and I'll come in a minute,' he said. 'I am just finishing here.' He gathered up papers, envelopes, and keys from the desk and went through to the rear office.

They were sitting on one of the sofas in the bay window of the lounge at the front of the hotel.

'I take you to Adalar, Princes' Islands this afternoon if you like? It will be good there—you can swim, and we can ride in the horse carts—no cars there.'

'That sounds good—OK, when does the boat leave? You don't have to work this afternoon?'

'I told you, I am manager—I can work when I want, I just keep everything OK with the staff and money and paperwork. I have to work now until about two o'clock, then we go, *tamam*?'

'OK love, that sounds fine—I'll go for a walk and come back then. See you later.'

They both stood up. Barbara reached up and kissed Mehmet's cheek, as she did so, she glanced over to the doorway—the man who had been on the terrace earlier, talking with Mehmet, was standing, watching them. Although she didn't know why, Barbara felt herself blush.

'This is Şerif, he is the brother of my . . . of one of my friends from college.'

Barbara went over to shake hands with the man, but he nodded at her curtly, turned rapidly and walked towards Reception, calling something to Mehmet in Turkish over his shoulder.

'What's wrong with him?'

'Oh don't worry, he is like that, I tell you about him later. I'm sorry if he is rude to you.'

'Well I don't think I've had a chance to do anything to upset him yet, have I? I mean, I've only just met the guy!'

'I must go now—enjoy your walk—you remember your way in Istanbul? You will be safe?'

'Don't worry, I'll be fine, I always am.'

FOUR

Out in the sunshine, Barbara walked over to the precincts of Sultan Ahmet and up to the grand main entrance to the mosque. She slipped off her sandals and gave them to the man standing waiting for them by the rows of pigeon-holed shelving. *'Funny job,'* she thought, *'Shoe Guardian.'* She thanked him and entered the mosque, loving the feeling of her bare feet on the richly-carpeted floor. *'Hello again'* she said silently to the hushed gorgeousness of the interior. She loved the colours, the tiles, the little candle-holders swinging gently on long, long, chains from way up in the dome.

But she felt she didn't want to linger there, today; she'd taken many photos in and around the mosque the previous year, and she had to admit that 'finding photographs' tended to be uppermost in her mind when in these sorts of surroundings. She took out her trusty old Konica and took a few shots of a huge, deeply carved door; then left through it; padded back across stone paving slabs to the 'Shoe Guardian'; retrieved her sandals; and set off towards the many-fountained area between the mosque and Aghia Sophia.

She sat at a table outside one of the little kiosk cafés and ordered an *elma chai*—apple tea, which arrived its tiny glass with tiny spoon and several sugar lumps balanced on the saucer.

She lit a cigarette and leaned back in her chair, 'grounding' herself in her surroundings. It seemed bizarre to have had that reminder of her life in Oxford—meeting Rosalind like that, and she mulled over recent months with Gareth. Since his illness had worsened, and their sex life had ceased, they had talked quite openly. 'I can't expect you to live like a nun,' he'd said to her.

And they'd kind-of agreed that so long as there was no 'excrement on their own doorstep', so to speak, that Barbara should get on with seeking sexual relationships elsewhere, if she wanted to. This all coincided with her exchange of letters with Mehmet, and as time went on, they grew more intimate, each acknowledging that there had been a 'spark' between them. So when he had suggested that she come back to Istanbul to see him, she had simply told Gareth what she intended to do, and he had simply said that a holiday would do her good.

When they first met, Mehmet had been studying at Beşiktaş University in Istanbul, but he had written first that he'd 'changed courses' and then that he'd left college, 'for a while', and had taken a job managing the hotel. He was keen to avoid having to do his National Service, from which he was excused while he was attached to a university. He now worried that unless he could take up his studies again, he would end up in the army, probably posted out to the Kurdish areas in the eastern part of the country. This horrified Barbara, who knew several Kurds back home in Oxford, and kept up with the political situation and alleged attacks by the Turkish army on Kurdish villages through her membership of Amnesty International. Mehmet's own opinion about the Kurdish independence movement surprised Barbara. He'd said: 'We all live in Turkey so we should all 'be Turkish''. Nevertheless, he had no desire to be a part of the harassment and atrocities going on in the east.

As she sat there, thinking, Barbara noticed that just next to her table, a man was sitting on a wooden box, deeply concentrating on what he was doing—was he painting? Sketching? He looked up and their eyes met.

He smiled and said: '*Merhaba*, hello, you are on holiday?'

'Yes,' she replied, 'well, I'm visiting a friend here. What are you doing?'

He held up a small square card, on which he had drawn the most beautiful calligraphic design.

'I am calligrapher—I have just returned from a big conference, very many artists in a competition and I came first in the whole contest!'

'Well done!'

'You are English?'

'Yes, I'm from Oxford.'

'Ah! Oxford University—a very fine place, very clever people there.'

'Well, yes, there certainly are some! But what are you doing out here?'

'I have a small bookshop but sometimes on nice days I come here and do these designs for the tourists, they seem to like them and I like doing them, it is practise for me.'

'You mean you sell them to tourists?'

'Sell them? No. I give them. I do not take money. But I meet many friends—now I have friends all over the world—I meet them like this and then they write me when they go home. Some of them come back to Istanbul many times. What is your name?'

'My name is Barbara,' she replied.

'My name is Salih. I will draw a design for your name and maybe we shall be also friends. Please write it for me here.' He passed her a notebook and a pencil and she wrote 'Barbara'.

'I'd like to come to your bookshop,' she said, as he began work. 'Where is it?'

'It is just behind the Bazaar, in the place that is called 'the book market' in Turkish—'Sahaflar Carsisi'—just by Beyazid Cami.'

'Oh—I've been there—last year!' Barbara said, 'In the beautiful little courtyard, there are many second-hand bookshops there.'

'Yes, old books. I sell old books and many old maps also. There! It is finished.'

'But you've only just started—oh it's so beautiful! How do you work so fast? That's fantastic!'

'When I win the contest some of it is for working fast, not only quality but for speed also. I will write my name and address on the back and then perhaps you will write to me from Oxford?'

'Of course. But I will come and see you at your shop later this week, too.'

Salih held out the card 'Here it is, my gift for you.'

'*Çok teşekkür ederim*—thank you very much.'

'Ah—you speak Turkish?'

'No, not really, I'm learning but not very good yet.'

'I must go to the shop now, I hope to see you again. I have been happy to talk with you.'

'It's been nice meeting you, and thank you again, it's really lovely. See you soon.'

Barbara returned to her seat and sat looking at the design on the card. Exquisite curls and swooping arcs of gold, red, green, and turquoise surrounded her name in elegant black ink in the centre. '*Yet another one of those 'things' that happen to me,*' she thought to herself. Throughout her life, Barbara had become aware that unusual and pleasant things happened to her unexpectedly. On holiday in The Lake District with her friend Jackie—the man who allowed them to take out a boat on Lake Coniston even though they had 'officially' closed for the day—and then didn't charge them; in Senegal, the lady from the Women's Group she had visited as part of her work who then delivered the gift of a beautiful hand-made *boubou*—the West African kaftan—to her hotel. And many, many more things besides. It was these experiences that convinced her that she would always be 'all right', that things would always work out for her no matter what.

She paid for her *chai* and strolled across the square, past the entrance to Aghia Sophia, the extravagant building that had been a church, then a mosque, and now a museum. The previous year, she and Gareth 'did' 'Ag Soph', learning about its complicated history and its fabulous mosaics. Gareth had done his usual 'homework' before the holiday and had drawn up a detailed itinerary of what they were to visit, when. It used to drive Barbara mad, feeling she was being 'frog-marched' through history. In Venice, with him, she ended up rising at six in the morning to go walkabout with her camera alone, to 'take in' what she wanted to about the place. She preferred to 'people watch', usually at cafés, while writing postcards. This was impossible to do if Gareth was with her. He would deign to stop for coffee sometimes, but would throw it down his throat and be ready for the off again before Barbara had time even to get out her address book and pen! Barbara heard someone on the radio once say that the difference between a tourist and a traveller is that a tourist, visiting a place, sees what they came to see; a traveller sees what's there. She liked that a lot.

She noticed a noisy little shop selling cassette tapes and vinyl LPs, and stopped to flip through cassettes in long, wooden boxes on wobbly-legged tables outside. They were extremely cheap, and she wondered if they were genuine or copies, '*Then again, at that price,*' she thought, '*who cares?*' She bought *The Cure*'s '*Wish*', which included that single she'd liked, '*It's Friday, I'm in Love*', and also *The Eurythmics: Greatest Hits*, and, noticing that it was already 1.30pm, made her way back to the hotel, where she wanted to put on her swimsuit under her clothes, to be ready for a dip at the Princes' Islands, later.

FIVE

'He is my mother's brother,' Mehmet said. They were on the ferry to Buyukada, the largest of the Princes' Islands and Barbara had told him about meeting Salih and showed him the calligraphic design of her name.

'Really? How strange.' She replied. 'He seems a nice man, I'd like to see his bookshop while I'm here. Then again, perhaps it was one of the ones I went into last year, we spent quite long time up there, it's such a lovely peaceful little area, especially when you've just taken on the Grand Bazaar itself!'

Mehmet laughed, 'That is true,' he said. 'Did you tell him you live in Oxford? He would like that!'

'Yes, why would he like that?'

'He is very intellectual and likes to meet intelligent people, students and professors.'

'Oh dear,' said Barbara, 'I'd better not tell him that my degree is from Oxford Polytechnic and not the University 'proper!'

'Does that matter? He would still be impressed!'

The ferry arrived and they walked from the jetty to a dusty main square, strewn with bits of hay and straw. A few market stalls selling tourist 'tat' and others selling fruit and vegetables. Many horse-drawn two- and four-wheeled carriages waited at one side of the square. Thin, scruffy-looking horses chomped at their nose-bags, flicking their tails at flies; stamping; jingling their harness.

They climbed aboard one after Mehmet had spoken to the 'driver'.

'We are going to the best place, best beach, it is very small and the tourists do not know it.' Barbara had taken photos of the square and the horses, and was still holding her camera. Mehmet reached for it 'Let me take your photo,' he said. He took several, looking terribly serious in his concentration as he operated the camera. The carriage stopped in a small lane, lined with hedges full of bright pink bougainvillea flowers. Mehmet paid the driver, who clicked his tongue at the horse and they clopped away, the sound of its unshod hooves receding softly.

'Come on,' said Mehmet, taking her hand and leading her through a small gap in the hedge and down a steep footpath overlooking a tiny bay. They scrambled down to the beach, a mixture of sand and shingle, edged with scrubby gorse bushes.

'Here you are, it is a private beach for us!'

'It's great,' she said, and walked away from him to the water's edge, sandals in hand, and let the waves lap over her feet.

When she turned around, Mehmet was taking things from his duffle bag, and laying them on a large piece of material he'd placed on the ground. She returned to him and he looked up, obviously pleased with himself.

'You brought lunch for us, how lovely!' she said. He had brought olives, a loaf of flat bread, tomatoes, and some pâté from the hotel kitchen, along with a couple of bottles of beer, china plates, and cutlery.

'That lot must have been heavy for you to carry,' she said.

'It's no problem, I wanted to have nice things to eat with you.'

As they ate, they chatted, making plans for the rest of Barbara's visit, Mehmet telling her when he had to work and when he would be able to spend time with her.

'Mehmet, that man, at the hotel, tell me about him, you said you would.'

'Şerif? What do you want to know about him?'

'Well, why he was so rude to me for a start.'

Mehmet, who had been leaning back on one elbow, sat up, cross-legged. 'I was at the University, you know. When I was there I have a girlfriend, Gul. He is her brother.'

'So he is rude to me because you finished with her? Does she still want to be with you? Is she still studying there?'

'Yes, she is still a student. But I didn't finish with her. I stopped seeing her when I left my course—when you met me—I was travelling for three months, you remember? Trying to get my head straight and decide what to do.'

'Yes, I remember you told me all that in your letters—go on.'

'When I get back to Istanbul, I started seeing her again, she is a very jealous woman, and she wants to get married and have children with me!'

'Ah, I see. So she is still your girlfriend, is that what you're saying?'

'She is more serious about it—I don't want to settle down—but yes, I still see her—we have sex, but not much now.'

'Did you tell her I was coming to Istanbul?'

'Yes—but first I tell her that I cannot see her this week. I said that you were important to me and you were coming to see me because you and your husband were unhappy.'

'For Christ's sake, Mehmet, no wonder her brother's pissed off with me! What did she say when you told her that?'

'She went mad—we were in the "Oxygen" club. She slapped my face and told all our friends there I was a bastard who fucked tourists! This is not fair because I told her how I met you with your husband and that it was only a bus journey!'

'I don't think she believed you, do you? So now what?'

'What do you mean?'

'Well is it over between you now? When did you tell her about me coming to see you? You never mentioned her in your letters.'

'I didn't say about her in letters because I told you, for me it is not important relationship, only for her it is. I told her last week.'

'LAST WEEK? Nothing like letting her down gently then! I don't think you treated her very nicely, by the sound of it. Have you seen her since she slapped you?'

'Yes, she came to the hotel the next day, and she keeps coming. I told her sorry she was upset but I never wanted serious relationship. She tries to force me to be with her, to love her. But I don't. She shouted—she said she would kill herself if I did not go back with her. And this she told her brother also!'

'Geez, what a mess! I feel really awkward now. I suppose all the people I've met so far—Atila, Osman—they know about all this?'

'Yes, but there is no need for you to worry about it. I will deal with it when you have gone back home.'

'I'm not worried about it, but it makes me feel—I don't know— different, that's all. I feel like "the other woman" and not as, well, not as free to enjoy being here, with all that going on.'

'She will not come to the hotel while you are here, this week. I asked her not to and she said she would not come.'

'But her surly brother is there quite often, isn't he?'

'I will talk to him, and we will enjoy this time together, it is only a short time and it is not like you are living in Istanbul.'

'Hmm . . . I wish it hadn't been like that between you. And I'm sorry there's all this hassle going on. And I wish you'd told me about her before now. But I'm here now, so not a lot I can do about it. I'm going for a swim.' And with that, Barbara pulled off her t-shirt, stepped out of her jeans, and ran down to the sea in her swimsuit.

The beach shelved steeply straight away, so Barbara was able to swim immediately she was in the water, without any of that tedious wading out and getting wet bit by bit. She struck out away from the beach, an efficient crawl stroke, cutting through the water. She was a strong swimmer, having been taught at a very early age by her mother, who used to say to family friends, 'I may not have been able to give my children very much, but at least I taught them all to swim!' Barbara had represented her schools at swimming competitions and galas, which she had not enjoyed at all, and the experience left her with a loathing of swimming pools, especially indoor ones. As an adult, she only ever swam in the sea.

She turned on her back and floated there, looking straight up at the cloudless blue sky. *'Oh shit!'* she thought. *'There's me feeling all "uncomplicated"—thinking I was getting away from "relationship angst" for a while and there's more of it here—in spades! Aye well.'* She wondered about Mehmet—her feelings for him. Was it just lust—was that what the 'spark' between them had been when they met? She really didn't think so, but what else could it be? There was no 'future' in their relationship—it was no different to 'holiday passions' experienced by thousands of women every year. Yet she flinched to think of herself bracketed with such women, and knew it was snobbish to feel superior to them, but she did.

She rolled in the water several times, she liked to do this—what she called 'seal rolling', and then headed back to the shore; to Mehmet; and to whatever the rest of the week might bring.

SIX

Mehmet had arranged for the same carriage to meet them up on the road at 4pm, and it was there waiting as they stepped out from the gap in the hedge. They had spent the afternoon talking—just talking. They had kissed a couple of times, but tenderly, not with the passion of the night before. Barbara went for another swim, and they had walked along the edge of the waves together, making up stories about the various flotsam and jetsam deposited there by the sea—bits of plastic, mainly, but also a shoe, a water bottle, the head of a doll, a bit of fishing net, a dead fish.

On the return ferry, Barbara felt tired and a little sunburnt—it was easy to forget how easy it was to 'overdo it'—especially near water, in this part of the world. So when they got back to the hotel, she went up to her room and had a cool shower before falling asleep on her bed. She set her travel alarm clock for 6pm, as Mehmet had the evening off and wanted to take her to dinner at Kumkapi—an area by one of the old city gates—famous for its many fish restaurants.

Mehmet had ordered a taxi, (not Atila's), and now, as they sat in the back, she looked at him, thinking how handsome he looked. He'd put on a very white shirt, a black linen jacket, and was wearing what looked like very new jeans. *'Tamam*—OK?' He asked her.

'Yes, I'm OK. I'm quite hungry—looking forward to dinner. How about you?'

'Yes, me too. I hope you like Kumkapi—I come here on my own

sometimes, many tourists come to eat, but not any of my friends, so I can be lost if I want to be alone.'

The taxi stopped on a busy dual carriageway; the sea on one side, huge city walls on the other. '*Haydi*—come on,' Mehmet said, 'This is it.'

He took her hand and they crossed the road, huge lorries charged past, other taxis bipped their horns at them—asking if they wanted to hire them. Once safely on the 'wall' side, Mehmet led her through an enormous gateway and into a pedestrianised square, chock-full of people seated at parasoled tables, waiters wove between them, holding trays aloft. Strangely, the traffic could no longer be heard; instead, the low murmur of many conversations, laughter, the occasional 'whoop' or cheer.

'It's great!' said Barbara, 'It's like walking onto a film set, after that horrible road out there!'

All of the restaurants were around the edge of the square, their tables arranged in individual groups, but the divisions between them obvious only to the waiters and other staff. Most of them didn't have seating inside—the only people to go in and out of the doors were the waiters on their way to and from the kitchens, fetching orders. When not 'on the move', waiters and kitchen staff stood in the door-ways, keeping watch on their tables, ready to be summoned by the diners.

Mehmet ordered for them both, 'It is local fish, very good,' he said. Side orders of tomato salad and chips. Barbara chose a bottle of red wine. As they ate, Mehmet told her about how he'd been feeling restless, during his last year at college. 'Many people they do not understand me; they say I think about too many things, I worry about the world. They are like—wearing horse's glasses.'

'What? What on earth do you mean?'

Mehmet gestured with his hands up by his eyes—'People do not want to see what is going on, really,' he said.

'Oh you mean BLINKERS! People have a 'blinkered view' of things, is that what you mean?'

'Yes, that's it, blinkers.'

'Oh I love that—'horse's glasses', that's fabulous!'

'You make fun of me.'

'No, oh Mehmet, no, I wasn't making fun of you—I think it's a lovely description, that's all. You know what I'm like about words. It's exactly what blinkers are—they ARE glasses for horses! Come on, cheer up, I didn't mean to upset you.'

'OK, but I was trying to be serious with you. I want you to know about me.'

'All right, I will listen and not interrupt you unless I don't understand something. But your expressions are part of my getting to know you as well, aren't they?'

He talked of how, in his first year at university, other students, and some tutors, thought he was 'obviously gay', simply because he liked to wear pink shirts at that time. Barbara thought of Gareth, and his fey, if not downright 'camp' mannerisms; then looked across at the hunk of Turkish masculinity sitting opposite her, and could not believe how these people had decided Mehmet's sexuality on the colour of his shirts! But she did not interrupt him. It was clear that he was 'pouring it all out' and needed her, or anyone, really, to listen while he did so.

'I am not talking like this when you are not here,' he took her hand when he said this. 'I don't know why it is but there is no-one I talk to, even long-time friends.' He told her how his father had left his mother and gone to live in a tiny apartment out near the airport. His mother had been lost in grief and gone, with her very old mother, Mehmet's grandmother, back to her home village, way out in Anatolia. Mehmet hardly got to see her anymore. He and his younger brother lived for about a month with their father, but it became impossible—he started drinking heavily, and brought 'loud' women back to the apartment. Mehmet was relieved to get the job at the hotel, he said, which gave him at least a room of his own. He left very few of his belongings behind at his father's place. His brother, Ali, was only fifteen, and Mehmet worried that he would 'become a criminal', by which Barbara took him to mean 'get in with the wrong sort', not having any parental guidance or discipline. But

Mehmet had arranged for Ali to live with the family of one of his school friends, and he was paying them a small amount every month for his brother's keep. 'So it is difficult,' he said. 'To not go in Army, I must be studying at University. If I stop, they take me. But if I am student, I do not have enough money for me and not any for my brother.'

It was getting late, although quite a few tables were still occupied, the waiters had longer to chat and smoke in the restaurants' doorways, where they had been joined by kitchen staff in their 'whites', some wearing chef's hats.

The noise of thunder had been rolling around for the past hour; people had looked up at the sky, anxiously, but then carried on chatting and eating. Now, the dark sky was lit up with tremendous forked lightning, accompanied by an incredibly loud ripping sound. Immediately, it started to rain. Huge drops hit their table, the debris of their meal within seconds was awash.

'Come on—quickly!' said Mehmet, grabbing Barbara's hand as she grabbed her cigarettes, lighter, and her bag.

They joined everyone else, running towards the restaurant doorways. The waiters waved them in, and then turned and held their trays on the floor, edge-on across the doorways, against what was becoming a torrent of rubbish-strewn water.

'Why don't they just close the doors?' Barbara shouted to Mehmet.

'They take them off—until they close at night, there are just the curtains,' he said. Barbara noticed that the doorways had only 'fly-screen' curtains, made of multi-coloured plastic strips, or thin metal chains. In some of the restaurants, men were trying to manoeuvre doors into place. Now and then, some of the marooned customers decided to make a break for it, and ran, ankle-deep, across the square to the road, hoping to hail a taxi, to shouts of 'Good luck!' from the other diners.

After twenty minutes, the scene out in the square was one of devastation. Water poured through and out of the gateway onto the dual carriageway. 'It's a flash-flood,' a young English guy was shouting. 'All the roads over there slope, look, and they all come into this square. The water can't go anywhere but through here and out over there!'

'I've never seen a thunderstorm start like that before,' said Barbara, 'only in films!'

A couple who had left earlier, in search of a taxi, returned, sloshing across to where they sheltered. 'No taxis out there,' the man said, 'just abandoned cars and people in the flats gawping out the windows at it all.' The rain was leaving off a little by now, and people seem to have given up any idea of staying dry, they stepped into the water and struggled off towards the road.

'What shall we do?' Barbara asked Mehmet.

'We wait and then we will go. It is not so bad as at first.'

'But it's like a river out there now—it's deep!'

'We will go now,' said Mehmet, and they shuffled to the front of the crowd and out into the square. 'We will go this way—I think we have to walk to hotel, and it is short way over here.' Mehmet held her hand, and had taken her bag and slung it over his shoulder. Everywhere, people called and beckoned to them from houses and apartments—offering shelter. Mehmet replied to them in Turkish and they carried on through filthy, muddy, water-filled streets and alleys.

Suddenly, they heard a car, coming up behind them, it was a VW Golf, a lovely, shiny, blue one, with German plates. 'Hey! Do you guys want a lift?' A woman was shouting from the passenger window. 'What a night, hey?' Barbara thanked them profusely and climbed into the back. As they drove, very slowly, through the floods, the woman turned and lent over the back of her seat, raising her voice to be heard and told them about themselves. They were Kiwis, Andy and Jo, working their way through the Med, she said, on an extended honeymoon—for six months. They'd picked up the car in Greece, and because they loved it, they were going to keep it for the whole trip. 'We should've bought a boat for this, though, eh?' Meanwhile, Mehmet was leaning forward at the back of Andy's seat, directing him. When they got to Aghia Sophia, he said 'This will be fine, thank you very much.' Andy stopped the car and Barbara thanked them again as she and Mehmet got out. They waved as the Golf crawled away again.

'What lovely people,' she said as they crossed the square, 'They really rescued us didn't they? Mehmet?' But Mehmet didn't respond. He was looking across at the hotel, at guests in their nightclothes helping to stack up chairs and cushions outside in the street.

SEVEN

Osman appeared and emptied a bucket of water into the stream that used to be the road outside the hotel. Mehmet ran towards him, shouting in Turkish. Inside, guests were gathering in the bar area, most in various states of undress, some with blankets around their shoulders, as they sat forlornly, bare feet tucked up under them. The whole area around the Reception desk was a mess. Part of the ceiling had collapsed, leaving a huge, ragged hole; lathes sticking out; plaster debris everywhere.

Barbara grabbed a bucket and something that could have been a bedspread, and started up the stairs, joining a young Turkish girl who was on all fours, mopping the floor on the first landing. She looked up at Barbara, 'Thank you, madam,' she said. A middle-aged man appeared from one of the rooms—'Miss, I say, MISS! Do you think we could get a hot drink? Tea? *Chai*? For my wife? . . . Oh God, Wendy, it's hopeless, they don't understand me,' he called back into the room, presumably to his wife. 'Yes, I do understand you, I'm English,' Barbara stood up and faced him. 'I'm sure that if you go down to the bar, someone will be making tea by now! If not, why not get some on the go? I'll be down when we've done this.' The man's face was a picture. He looked astonished. Barbara later realised that with her dark colouring, long skirt, and headscarf, how easily she could be taken for a Turkish woman. Obviously, the man had thought she worked at the hotel—why else would she be crawling about on the floor, clearing up? A woman's voice called out 'That's a *good* idea, Tom, let's get down there and see if we can help.' Barbara left them to it and followed the Turkish girl up to the next floor, mopping at the stairs one-by-one as she went.

It was now 3am. Barbara was sitting on a bar stool, cupping a mug of tea in her dirty, cold and wrinkled hands. The hotel staff were all in the dining room, with Mehmet, a couple of policemen, and a doctor who had arrived and asked if anyone was hurt. Thankfully, no-one was. The damage to the building wasn't actually all that bad, either. The roof had leaked, badly, in several places, mostly onto the stairwell, and the two rooms on the top floor. Barbara's room, being a recent addition to the roof terrace, had a new flat roof, and was completely dry and undamaged.

The door to Mehmet's room was open, but a huge pile of plasterboard and muck was piled up in the doorway. The Reception area, in front of his room, had been 'cordoned off' with plastic tape—probably care of the policemen. In the bar, Rosalind had been a brick—jollying people along, getting them all seated and sending Margaret, who looked a bit shell-shocked, running back and forth to fetch blankets. Hot tea was being provided by a woman Barbara presumed was 'Mrs Tom/Wendy', who was presiding at the counter. The policemen and doctor were leaving, Mehmet was standing with Osman, seeing them off. He ran his hand through his hair. Barbara was worried to see him so upset. She hopped off the stool and went over to him. He said nothing, simply put his arm around her and dropped his face onto the top of her head. Then he put out his other arm and laid it on Osman's shoulder. Osman looked at Barbara and said 'Oh dear. Bloodyhell.'

Luckily, only one of the damaged guest rooms had been occupied, and the couple from it had been moved to a vacant room on the first floor. By 4am, the guests had all gone to their rooms, the non-resident staff had gone home, leaving Mehmet, Osman, and Barbara in the bar. Mehmet had got down a bottle of brandy from the shelves behind the counter, and poured out three generous glasses. 'Şerife, cheers, poor hotel,' he said, raising his glass.

'At least no-one was hurt, *canim*,' Barbara said as she 'chinked' his glass with her own, 'I know that you were thinking the worst when we first saw it.'

'The worst? I think the hotel was collapsed—is it 'demolshed', the word?'

'Demolished, yes, completely destroyed. It was scary wasn't it?'

Osman took his glass and said he was going to lay down in his room. They said goodnight and Mehmet thanked him for all his help. 'I should have been here,' he said when he had gone. 'He was very good boy—he is only young boy but he was in charge.'

'He did very well, he knew what to do, and got everyone sorting it all out. God, but wasn't he glad to see you when we arrived!'

It was almost light outside, the birds were starting to sing. 'Another early-morning-late-night,' said Mehmet, stubbing out a cigarette.

'What will happen now, about the hotel, I mean?' she asked.

'The owner will come tomorrow. He will arrange about the repair— I hope he does not close hotel for making the repair.'

Barbara looked at Mehmet's worried face; his lovely black hair was covered in dust, making him look older, as if prematurely grey. His jacket was torn on one of the sleeves; his 'very white' shirt was filthy. 'Come on,' she said, 'Let's go to bed for a couple of hours at least.' She led him to the stairs where he hesitated. 'Well you won't be sleeping in there, will you?' she said, nodding at the mound of debris blocking the door to his room. Mehmet shrugged and smiled, 'No, you are right. It is not possible.' And he followed her up the stairs.

'Thank you for helping Zeliha,' he said as they went up. 'It was very kind of you.'

'Zeliha? Oh, the girl cleaning the stairs? That's OK. I thought it best to get the stairs cleared up so people could get to their rooms safely.' They arrived at the door to Barbara's room. He took the key she handed him, unlocked the door and they went in.

Barbara told him about the man asking her for tea, thinking she worked there, which made him laugh. 'I will give you job if you like,' he said.

'You couldn't afford me!'

Barbara pulled off her headscarf and shook it—sending a shower of dust over them. 'God, just look at us, will you?' She went to him and brushed at his jacket sleeve 'Shame about your jacket, here, take it off, I'll look at it tomorrow, I might be able to mend it.' She took the lapels in her hands, about to help him remove it. Mehmet stopped her by taking both her hands in his and holding them down level with her waist. 'Jacket can wait for mending, I need you to mend me,' he said. 'Need you very much.' And he kissed her. He was still kissing her as he let go her hands and shrugged out of his jacket and let it fall to the floor.

Barbara laughed and stepped back. They stood looking at each other for a moment, then Mehmet moved to the bed and sat on the edge, reaching for her, 'Come here, my cleaning woman, I will undress you.' She stood in front of him while he undid her skirt and removed it, kissing her stomach. She pulled her t-shirt over her head, throwing it to the growing pile of flood-damaged clothing on the floor, and took Mehmet's face in her hands. He stood up, and, holding her gaze the whole time, took off his shirt, then moved to her and undid her bra, letting her ample breasts fall. 'Beautiful. Waiting so long for you,' he said into her hair. Barbara felt the heat of his bare chest against her skin and was immediately more aroused than she would have thought possible at that time of day, after such a night of scivvying, and worrying for Mehmet—not the most romantic or passionate prelude to their first night together.

He was taking his time, however, slowly running his hands and his tongue over her body. He paused, while she was laying face down on the bed; he threw his wallet on the floor, and she realised he was putting on a condom. 'I brought some of those, you know, just in case I needed them.' she said.

'I have them also, so we will use them all, before you go home. Now turn over,' he pushed gently at her shoulder, so that she was face-down again.

She felt him stroking her thighs with his fingers, ever so lightly, and couldn't help moaning softly, it was wonderful. He drew his fingers across her buttocks, and then between her legs, only for a second, and then to her thighs again. Because she could not see him, behind her, she had no idea where he would touch her next, and the anticipation made his touch electric.

When he entered her, Barbara thought she would orgasm straight away, she was at such a pitch of excitement. He moved in strong, assertive thrusts inside her. She was trying not to make too much noise—crying out as she came, and then begging him to stop, it was all just too much, too exquisite, almost painful. He slowed his pace and moved very slowly into her as far as he could, then withdrew, then repeated the move, again, and again. Then he cried out, '*Evet! Evet* . . . yes!', digging his nails into her hips as he pulled her to him, thrusting hard against her as his orgasm shuddered through him. He laid forward and covered her body with his.

EIGHT

Barbara woke up alone, and as usual, freezing cold. She pulled the sheet up over herself and lay there, thinking. They'd had wonderful, enthusiastic sex before they fell asleep, exhausted. He'd been so tender, but assertive in his love-making. Kept saying how he'd waited so long to love her. She looked at her watch—nearly nine o'clock—she had not woken with the early-morning *ezans*—then she realised that they were probably in the middle of 'activities' at five am, having gone to her room when it was already daylight.

She thought about the night before, the flood; the damaged ceiling; the mess. And before, at Kumkapi, what Mehmet had told her about his life and his worries over being carted off to the army if he didn't take up his studies again; about his parents; about his brother. Then she remembered all about the 'Gul' business, his suicidal girlfriend with the grumpy brother.

'*But hey, on with the motley, and on with the show,*' she said to herself, got out of bed and went to have a shower.

Once dressed, she gathered up the pile of grubby clothes from the night before, noticing Mehmet had left his jacket and his shirt. The tiny sink in the shower room wouldn't be any use for rinsing clothes, so she decided she'd check out the hotel's 'backrooms', downstairs to see if she could wash them there. She shoved them all in a carrier bag and went down.

In the bar she found Osman, who smiled at her 'You like coffee?'

he asked. 'I was going to bring breakfast, but Mehmet said 'no'. I am sorry.'

'No, that's fine, Osman, don't worry. I was sleeping. I don't eat breakfast at home, anyway, just coffee.'

'No? You do not eat in morning? OK.' And he made busy with the rather cronky Gaggia machine. '*But it IS a proper Gaggia*', thought Barbara.

'Osman, is there somewhere where I can wash these clothes from last night?'

'Give them to me, I will get girl to do it.'

'No, you won't, they've all got too much to do clearing up after last night. Just show me where there is a sink and I will do it. I'm very domesticated you know—we don't have servants running around after us at home!'

'Mehmet will give me hard time if I let you do washing,' he said.

'Well, don't tell him then. Anyway,' she held up Mehmet's shirt, 'Some of it is his washing, so he should count himself lucky that I'm doing it for him!'

When she'd had her coffee and a cigarette, Osman showed her through the kitchens to a brick-built shed outside. There was a huge, chipped, white sink, a wooden draining board, and two rather rusty spin dryers. A couple of clothes lines were slung between posts to one side of the shed.

'You do not touch plug with . . . your hands are wet, you understand?' Osman indicated the flexes and two-pin plugs looped over the sockets hanging precariously from the wall.

'It's OK, I'll be careful. Thanks, Osman.'

She busied herself washing and rinsing out the clothes. She dabbed at Mehmet's jacket with a small sponge, but thought it looked worse afterwards; muddy streaks and white lines smeared down the front. She decided not to risk the spin dryers; it was a beautiful, warm day, so she located a plastic tub of pegs and hung the washing on the lines outside. A ginger and white cat watched her from the shade of a tree.

'*Merhaba, kedi*,' she said to it.

'It is Van cat, Turkish Van. Special cat to Turkey.'

Barbara started. It was Şerif, the 'surly brother-of-girlfriend'. He was standing, smoking a cigarette, in the doorway of the kitchen.

'Oh, Şerif, hello. You startled me.'

'I am sorry.' He threw his cigarette end away and moved towards her. 'And I am sorry also for before—when I meet you first.'

'Thank you. Er, look, Mehmet told me about Gul. I understand. But I didn't understand before . . . I mean . . . I didn't know he had a girlfriend. We have only written to each other and he didn't say he had a girlfriend, and . . .'

'It is all right. I talked to him this morning, it is not your fault. It is not anyone's fault. He does not love my sister. She loves him. Mehmet is my friend and I know him. He will not marry her. I don't know if he will marry at all.'

'Why do you say that?'

'Mehmet is a thinker. He thinks much but does not know what to do in life. One day, maybe, he will find what is right to do, for him.'

'Well, I hope so too, but I hope Gul is all right as well. I hope she will be happy.'

'She is young, only twenty-one years, she will get over it.'

Mehmet appeared behind Şerif, shielding his eyes from the sun with his hand.

'Tamam?' He looked from Barbara to Şerif and back again.

'Hello, yes, we've been chatting, we're OK. Şerif, I hope we can be friends?'

Şerif extended his hand and Barbara took it. 'Yes, we can.' He said, and smiled. Nodding towards Mehmet, he continued: 'But what is this, he has you working for him already, in hotel?' And he winked at her, let go her hand, and strode back into the kitchen, patting Mehmet's shoulder as he passed him.

'You OK? What was he saying to you? Are you all right?'

'Yes, I told you. He apologised for being rude. He said you talked this morning. Where have you been?'

'The owner came. My boss. We went to his other hotel—no mess there—to talk. It is not so bad, men will come tomorrow to fix roof

45

and all the rest of it. We have to ask all the guests if they want to change hotel—they can go to other one if they like.'

'That's good. I'm not going anywhere though, I'd rather stay here!'

He smiled and put his arm around her. 'But listen, *canim*, the English women you know, something bad has happened.'

'Rosalind and Margaret? What? What has happened?'

'There was phone call from England earlier this morning. I took it and had to wake them. The lady's husband—he died.'

NINE

Rosalind was sitting in the front room of the hotel, on a sofa. Margaret sat next to her, looking tearful. Barbara went in and took Rosalind's hands: 'I'm so, so, sorry to hear . . .' she began.

'It's quite all right, dear,' Rosalind said, 'When one's spouse is so much older, one has to be prepared for this. I was his student, you know, when we met. He would have been ninety in September.'

Margaret started to cry. 'Now come on, Mags, it's all right. There now, there, there.' Rosalind patted Margaret's arm and gave her a handkerchief.

'What will you do now?' Barbara asked.

'Well, I have been on the phone all morning, as you can imagine,' said Rosalind. 'I'm going to go home tomorrow—funeral arrangements and all sorts to attend to. But I'd prefer it if Mags stayed here until the weekend, no need for her to leave yet. And it will be ghastly, going through it all, without having to worry her with it too.'

'But you need some support,' Margaret whimpered. 'I can help you, can't I?'

'I appreciate that you want to be there for me, dear, but the best way you can 'support' me, really, is if you stay here until the weekend. We can arrange a flight for you for then, and that will give me just a little space to organise things. Will you do that for me, please?'

'But I'll be on my own here, worrying about you' said Margaret. 'But I suppose I'll be OK. I mean, of course I will, I didn't mean to be selfish, sorry.'

'Well, look, Mags—can I call you that? I'm here until Friday night, and you know me. And we can go places together, when Mehmet's working. With all the flood damage, he's probably going to be tied up with that and . . .' her words dried up as she realised what she'd said. She'd 'given the game away' about her relationship with Mehmet. She looked at Rosalind.

'There you are then, you see? You two will be company for one another.'

And she winked at Barbara. This woman, in the chaotic midst of bereavement, actually winked at her, her eyes smiling. 'And I think he's a dish,' she said to Barbara, quietly. 'Well done you!'

'That's kind of you,' Mags was saying, between sniffling into her hanky. She turned to Rosalind: 'If you're sure that's what you want, my love, I'll stay.'

'Good girl! That's better. Now, what about some lunch?'

The two women left the hotel arm in arm. Barbara watched them through the bay window, sitting on the deep sill, her knees up to her chin.

'Are they all right?' It was Mehmet, who walked over and perched on the arm of the sofa nearest to Barbara.

'Yes, far more "all right" than you can imagine, especially Rosalind,' She said. 'She knows about us, I gave it away, but I think she knew anyway.'

'How do you know? What did you say?'

'Oh, it doesn't really matter, but she thinks you're 'a dish'!'

'This woman has husband who died yesterday and she says that?'

'He was very old, I told you that. He was ninety, nearly, and she said she had been prepared for it. She's only in her fifties, I should think.'

Mehmet blew out a long breath, holding his hands up then dropping his palms onto his thighs as he rose: 'Puuuuh, it is strange to me,'

'But listen, Rosalind's going home tomorrow, back to Oxford. But Mags—her friend, Margaret—she's staying here until Saturday. I said I'd take her out a bit, that I could do with her company while you were working. Although that's not true, you know I enjoy wandering about on my own.'

'I see. That is why they know—you say you wait for me to not work—to be together?'

'Exactly. But it's fine. It's better than 'fine'. I feel better about everything today—sorry for her loss and all the hassle that poor Rosalind has to go through now, but as for me, I've made proper friends with the two of them. I think we shall see each other in Oxford. Oh God!—I expect Gareth knows about Henry's death, or he will soon. I expect he'll go to the funeral. I'll probably go with him. Hey—what about Şerif then? He's my friend now, as well!'

'He's OK. He tells me he is worried about his sister, that is all. But it will be all right. Do you want a drink?'

They went to the bar and Mehmet got her a Coke. Several of the guests were in there, and nodded and smiled at them. 'No-one is going to leave,' Mehmet said. 'They all are very nice about the problem and they say they will stay—the repair will take one day only.'

He leant over the counter to her and spoke quietly: 'Last night—I don't know how to say . . . it was special, fantastic. I knew it would be like this, when I first meet you. I'm sorry I left you but you were sleeping. I had to meet my boss.'

'That's OK love. There's so much going on, apart from "us", isn't there? It's only Sunday and it's been quite an adventure. And yes,' she said, touching his hand, 'Last night was fantastic.'

Later that day, Barbara went to Rosalind and Mags' room to talk to them while Rosalind packed. She went to reassure Mags, really, as the poor woman was still wobbly and tearful.

Barbara watched Rosalind as they talked—the stereotypical 'good sort' of intellectual, liberal Englishwoman. Eccentric in a 'no-nonsense' kind of way, if that made sense. Nothing much could shock them; they had no known enemies and many friends. More likely to know about the living conditions in the shanties of Guatemala than on the council estates in Oxford's suburbs, but entirely without snobbery. Prepared always to give anyone a chance, so long as they were polite and sincere. It was people just like Rosalind whom Barbara had begun to encounter when, aged twelve, she and her mother moved to Oxford. And she so aspired to be one of them.

Barbara's father had been sixty-two years old when she was born—her mother thirty-two. He was Irish, and had met Barbara's mother when she was working, to the shame of her clergyman father, in a pub, having been deserted with two young children, by her naval-officer husband. From what Barbara could gather from her half-siblings, her father had a bookshop in Gosport, and a little old Irish wife too. But her father left his wife and took off to Oxfordshire with Barbara's mother, and there she was conceived, in rooms rented from the woman who became Barbara's god-mother. They rented a large house in a lovely village, where Barbara was born. Her half-siblings came to join them, and they had been happy, though fairly poor, until the day Barbara's father died, when she was seven years old.

By this time, Barbara's half-sister was married, and her brother in the Navy and about to be married himself. After five years 'in limbo', in a council house, her mother got a job as warden of an old people's home in Oxford, and she and Barbara moved into the warden's flat. Barbara *loved* Oxford. She said that it 'ruined her' for living anywhere else. Oxford satisfied her thirst for knowledge, for culture, for history. Her cosmopolitan 'city of learning' made it possible for her to believe that she could 'cross the divide'—from council-house kid to middle-class, academic, adulthood. The greatest day of her life, so far, was her graduation day, as a 'mature student' aged twenty-eight, at which her mother had told her 'Your father would have been so proud of you.' Barbara was pretty pleased, herself, with an Upper Second in English/Anthropology/History—'Social Studies' sounded so dull, so she always told people her subjects, if they asked. She became 'politically aware' at college—playing leading roles in the Anti-Apartheid Society and in the Amnesty Group. It was the happiest time—she couldn't believe that she was being 'allowed' to do nothing for three years except learn, read, and mix with like-minded people. OK, her 'alma mater' was Oxford Polytechnic, not the 'University proper', but the hell with it, she was an undergraduate.

Probably because she had been so young when he died, Barbara developed a strong interest in her father's family, and Irish culture and history along with it. She read Irish literature and began frequenting, and then singing at local folk clubs; found she didn't have a bad voice; and could hold a tune. As a result of this immersion in 'things Irish', she would often find herself using words and little phrases, and structuring her sentences as someone from Ireland would do. She liked to do this, she thought of it as a mark of respect, and love, for her late father.

She met Gareth just after she graduated, at an Amnesty street vigil at Carfax, at the top of Queen's Street. They started chatting and she was attracted by his cutting sarcasm and deeply-referenced conversation—she 'got' his obscure references—to literature, film, politics. He was tall, not terribly good-looking, but he, like her, was the first in his family to get a degree, and she liked sharing that with him. They married quickly, only three months later, and had a lovely wedding party after the Registry Office formalities, at the large flat they rented—the ground floor of a quirky old house—on leafy and expensive Headington Hill. Then Gareth became ill. He was cantankerous and difficult to live with from the start, but he got worse. They never went out anywhere, and he resented it if Barbara went out without him, so she stopped doing so. When she landed the job she so wanted, as a researcher at a development agency, he was pleased for her, but hated it when she went away for her work. They took a few holidays, and then the last one, to Turkey, before he started dialysis, and on which she met Mehmet.

'Penny for them, dear,' Rosalind waved a folded map in front of Barbara's face.

'Oh, sorry, miles away.'

'I could see that. Will you join us for our 'last supper' tonight?— That sounds dreadful, doesn't it? Why don't you bring your nice young man too?'

Barbara felt her face flush. 'Well, if you don't mind, I mean, are you sure? I'll ask him—Mehmet—I'd like to.'

'Good. We're going to The Roof Garden next door—oh goodness, I hope they weren't flooded out last night as well.'

'No, they're fine, Mehmet saw one of the guys who works there this morning.'

'Right you are then, why don't you meet us up there at eight?'

'Thank you, I'm sure we will. I'll go and check it out with him now.' She left them fussing over which socks were whose, and went downstairs.

Mehmet and Osman were using huge shovels to push all the broken plasterboard and rubbish in the Reception area to one side, they wore scruffy, ripped t-shirts and holey, paint-smeared jeans. They looked gorgeously 'physical'.

'I thought you said the workmen were coming tomorrow!' Barbara called to them. 'Do you want a cold drink?'

Mehmet stopped what he was doing and swept his forearm across his forehead. 'Yes, please, cold beer would be great. Thank you.'

'Osman drinks beer as well?' She said, eyebrows raised.

'Yes, most of us do—I told you when you asked me in letters. For most of us being Muslim is like when your Catholics say they are 'Catholic' without sticking to much of what that is meant to mean!'

'OK,' she laughed, 'only asking!'

She opened a couple of bottles of *Efes* from the fridge in the bar and took them back to Mehmet and Osman.

'Do you want to go to dinner with Rosalind and Margaret tonight, Mehmet? They've invited us.'

'They invite me as well?

'Yes, Rosalind did. What do you think?'

'If you want to, yes, I am happy.'

She left them to their labours and went to her room, stopping by to tell Rosalind they would be happy to join them later.

TEN

Barbara had done her best to mend Mehmet's jacket, but it was beyond the scope of her 'travel sewing kit', really. Mehmet came to her room to shower and change before meeting the two women for dinner. 'Sure, look, you can roll back the sleeves—it's a bit 'Eighties', but it'll do!' she laughed as she turned the sleeves for him.

The Roof Garden looked like fairyland—tiny white lights twinkled among the trailing vines and huge potted palms. Any hesitation that Barbara had felt about spending the evening with Rosalind and Mags disappeared as they all chatted, laughed, ate. Rosalind 'held court', telling tales of her travels; of field trips with Henry when they were first married. In far better Turkish than Barbara's, she asked Mehmet about himself, his family, his life in Istanbul, but then would drop back into English so that Mags and Barbara would not feel excluded or awkward. It was a lovely evening, although Barbara felt guilty for feeling so happy every time she remembered Rosalind's bereavement.

At around ten o'clock, Rosalind pushed back her chair and said that she and Mags should turn in, as she had an early start for the airport next morning. Barbara and Mehmet stood up and made to collect their things together too.

'No my dears, there's no need for you to leave,' said Rosalind. 'You stay and finish that wine, shame to waste it.'

'But we need to pay the bill,' Barbara said, looking towards the waiters at the bar.

'It's all taken care of, dear. No, I insist. We were very glad of your company and I invited you. My treat. Now say no more about it.'

'It's so kind of you, thank you. Shall I see you in the morning? What time are you leaving?'

Mehmet interrupted: 'Atila is coming with taxi at six o'clock.'

'Well, I'm usually awake by then, so I'll come down to see you off,' said Barbara, as she embraced Rosalind. 'Mags, then you and I can have 'early morning tea'—I'll make it for us.'

The ever-attentive waiters escorted the ladies carefully down the wooden staircase; one of them accompanying them back to The Meydan, next door.

Barbara looked at Mehmet, who was chatting to a couple of his friends who worked at The Roof Garden. She smiled to herself. He had been so charming all evening, so polite. When they arrived and when they left, he had kissed Rosalind's and Mag's hands. He had captivated Rosalind completely, who already thought he was 'a dish', of course.

'Why are you smiling?' He came back to their table, carrying a bottle of brandy and two glasses.

'Oh, just thinking what a nice evening it's been. I wondered how it would be, with Rosalind's news, I mean, but it was so lovely to chat and relax with them.'

'They are nice women. Very intelligent. Rosalind is like my university professors. And she is strong woman, too, I think.'

'Yes, I think you're right. She will get back to Oxford and just get on with things that need to be done.' They drank the rest of the wine; then a couple of brandies with coffee, talking all the time about the conversation over dinner with the two women.

Finally, when they realised they were the only customers left, Mehmet called his friends over to join them for a cigarette, before he and Barbara left, and his friends finished clearing up for the evening.

On their return to the hotel, they went up to Barbara's room straight away; it seemed the natural thing to do, not requiring discussion or hesitation this time. They undressed, kissing one another's bodies. But they had each drunk more than they were used to, and as soon as they laid down and covered themselves with the drowsy warmth of the duvet, they fell asleep; Barbara's head on Mehmet's chest; his arm around her.

'Mehmet? What time is it?' He was picking up clothes, stepping into his jeans.

'It's five-thirty—I remembered to set alarm on my watch.'

'Well done, I don't know about you, but I think I'd have overslept, we put away quite a lot of wine last night didn't we?'

'And brandy!'

'Yes, and the brandy—nice, though!' She got out of bed and went into the shower room.

'No hot water, too early. Later you have shower.'

'Oh shit! Never mind, there's not really time, anyway.'

Mehmet left her to dress and went down to open the front door, he went into the street and smoked a cigarette while he waited for his cousin to arrive in his taxi. Rosalind opened the door of her room just as Barbara was coming down the stairs, and the two of them carried her case down; a silent Mags came after them, holding Rosalind's handbag. When Mehmet saw them, he ran into the hotel, 'Here! Here! I will take it! You should tell me—I should take bag!' Everyone was whispering, but he still managed to sound urgent.

'That's all right, we managed, dear. Now, we'll just sit here, Mags, let me have my bag, please.'

Mags sat next to Rosalind, entreating her to telephone the hotel as soon as she could, when she got home; pulling at a handkerchief balled up in her hand. Then all at once, Atila was there; the case loaded into the boot of the taxi, everyone hugged, and Rosalind was gone. Mags looked after the car until it was out of sight, then she turned, let out a great sob, and crying bitterly, allowed herself to be led gently into the lounge.

Barbara sat with her on a sofa, while Mehmet went to make tea. She whimpered like a small puppy. She would apologise, sniffle into her hanky, and try to pull herself together, but each attempt was short-lived. She would bend forward again, leaning over her knees, rocking and sobbing. Mehmet brought the tea on a tray. He looked worried and a little embarrassed.

'Hey love, I think we could do with some brandy again,' Barbara said, and he disappeared again to the bar.

It was almost an hour before Mags was breathing calmly again.

'All cried out, for now,' she said. 'Thank you so much for being with me, for the tea and everything. You're very kind.'

'Well, we couldn't have you creeping about, all upset at this hour, could we? You didn't know where the brandy is kept, anyway!' Mags managed a weak smile, and said she would go to her room and try to sleep a bit longer.

Barbara took the tray out to the bar, where she found Mehmet. Osman and a couple of women were busy preparing breakfast dishes and laying tables.

'Poor love,' she said. 'She's in pieces. And exhausted—she's gone to her room for a sleep.'

'It is best, for her,' said Mehmet. 'She will sleep now and be better later.'

'I'm going to try for a shower now—are you OK?'

'Me? Yes, I'm OK. But I need a shower too,' he leant towards her, 'Can I have shower with you?' He grinned cheekily.

'Saving water, is it? Come on then!'

ELEVEN

Given that the hotel guests were assembling for their breakfasts; and it was Monday morning—a busy day with expected arrivals and planned departures; Barbara felt slightly guilty at keeping the Hotel Manager from his duties. But that was the only reason for her guilt, and it was only slight. They had clung together, kissing passionately, under the shower. Then Mehmet had towelled her hair, and seated on the edge of the bed, he had pulled her onto him and they made love, quickly and noisily.

'I'm sure this isn't in your job description,' she laughed as they dressed. 'Unless it's something to do with "customer satisfaction"!'

'You do not think I do this with other guests?' Mehmet once again looked hurt.

'No, love, I was joking. Not serious, OK?'

'OK, but I do not want you to think . . .'

She cut him off: 'And I don't. So stop it. Come on, you're supposed to be working and I want some breakfast!'

Later that morning, Barbara wandered over to the Archaeological Museum gardens and sat at a café table for a couple of hours, drinking *chai*, smoking, and writing a few postcards she'd bought at the kiosk. She found it hard to believe it was only Monday.

And then it was Thursday. She was sitting at the same café table; this time with Mags.

'I can't believe I'm going home tomorrow,' she said. 'Where did the week go?'

Mags put down her book: 'Well, we can't say that it hasn't been eventful,' she said. 'I'm really grateful to you for taking me all over the place with you. That's why it's gone so quickly, I expect. And I'm so pleased that we've got to know each other. I hope we'll be friends back in Oxford, too?'

Barbara found herself saying: 'Yes, I'm sure we will,' but wondering how likely it was. They moved in different circles, and she couldn't help feeling envious of Mags' 'work-when-you-feel-like-it' lifestyle', which allowed her to travel, write, and study as she pleased. She had admitted to Barbara that except for a small amount of money she'd inherited on her father's death, she had 'no money at all' and that Rosalind was 'keeping her'—she lived in Rosalind's huge house in North Oxford rent-free. They each had their own rooms.

She had been remarkably frank in telling Barbara about her relationship with Rosalind.

'I know that people think we're lesbians,' she had said quite suddenly as they walked through Gulhane Park a couple of days previously. 'But I'm not sure that we really *are*? I mean, sometimes we sleep in the same bed, like when we're here, when we're travelling, but . . . What I mean is, we don't, you know . . . we don't have a *sexual* relationship. Never have.'

Barbara had felt uncomfortable with this information; she really didn't care whether they had sex or not. And she certainly didn't think it was the place for Mags to bimble along, wittering away about her sex life, or lack of it, among all the tourists—and even the locals—who could understand at least the words 'lesbian' and 'sex'!

'I think of you as "companions",' she said to Mags, as she steered her into a quieter area of the park. 'And there's nothing wrong with that, is there? As long as you both are happy with your situation, and your relationship, who cares what people think? And I'm sure you know that you're not *at all* unusual back in our dear Oxford!'

One afternoon, they had gone with Mehmet to the second-hand book market and visited Salih in his shop—which was, Barbara remembered, the one in which she'd bought some 'vintage' lapel badges the year before. Salih made them tea, and did a calligraphed card with the name 'Margaret', for Mags, who was as charmed by him as Barbara had been when first they met. Salih had seemed very pleased that Barbara was a friend of Mehmet's. The two men talked at length in their own language while Barbara and Mags browsed the shelves. Salih asked Barbara many questions about herself, and about her life in Oxford. He asked her to visit him again whenever she was back in Istanbul, and asked if she would she write to him now and then.

On the Wednesday evening, they had been to a wedding party—over the Bosphorus in Kadikoy. It was yet another cousin of Mehmet's, a tall, thin young man called Irem, who had been married the week before, and 'everyone was invited', Mehmet said. They were the only 'foreigners' there and were fussed over by everyone. The younger women insisted on trying to teach them how to belly-dance, and then announced to Barbara's embarrassment that she was rather good at it, 'Like Turkish woman,' they'd said, giggling and looking over at Mehmet, who was standing with his male relatives.

So now here they were. Thursday. Barbara due to fly home the next morning.

Mehmet and Barbara went back to The Roof Garden that night, for a meal together. 'My treat this time,' Barbara told him. They had invited Mags, but she declined, partly, Barbara thought, to give them time alone on her last night, but also, she had befriended a German couple who were staying at the hotel, and was going to eat out with them that night.

'You are sure you do not want me to come to airport tomorrow?' Mehmet asked, as he poured Barbara a brandy after dinner.

'It's going to be hard enough as it is, leaving you, so it's best, believe me, that you don't come. If I can just get on with all the usual 'processing' that goes on at airports, I'll be fine. It'll take my mind off you.'

'We can walk around for a little while, do you mind?' Mehmet asked as they left the restaurant.

'No, of course I don't mind. It's such a lovely night. I've packed everything I can, anyway—I wanted to keep tonight free—for us.' She took his hand and Mehmet raised it to his lips and kissed it.

They skirted the square between Sultan Ahmet and Aghia Sophia, and walked down through the old Hippodrome area. As they crossed the road, Barbara noticed a flashing neon sign: 'Oxygen'. 'Oh, is that the club you told me about—where you were with Gul before I arrived?'

'Yes, that is it. Do you want to go there?'

'Not particularly—do you?'

'It is loud in there, but there is a small garden at the back. We could have coffee there maybe?'

Barbara felt that he wanted to go there with her. Perhaps it was some sort of 'laying a ghost', for him—so that he'd have happier memories of the place—instead of it being the place where his girl-friend had slapped and humiliated him.

'OK, but I don't really like clubs, you know. Let's not stay long.'

The garden at the back was lovely. Instead of the insistent 'doof-doof' beat of the music, it was full of the sound of water, from little chan-nels and streams running around the patio. They drank their coffee and smoked, discussing details of her departure the next morning. Mehmet stroked Barbara's cheek: 'It has been so . . . right—to have you here,' he said. 'I hope you will come again soon. Please?'

'I have some thinking to do, love. Sure, I've almost forgotten that I've a husband and a job back home. Maybe that might change. I just don't know where my life is supposed to be going at the moment.'

'I know you have difficult time. But you think we are good together? I am thinking: 'Could we be together one day?' But I have many difficulties and have to make decisions, too. I may not be able to stay in Turkey—if I do they will take me to the army.'

'I know. Let's not talk about it all again now, not on my last night. Let's go back.'

As they pushed through the crowded bar, suddenly, Barbara saw Osman, standing with a group of young men and women, obviously his friends. 'Mehmet, look—there's Osman, over there.' And she raised her arm to wave across the room at him.

'No, leave him, we will go now.' Mehmet grabbed her hand and made for the door.

'What's wrong?' she asked him.

'It is nothing. It is . . . the woman with blonde hair next to him . . . that is Gul.'

Barbara looked back and saw that Osman and his friends had seen them. He had his hand on the arm of a short, plump girl, who had the stereotypical 'yellow-blonde' dyed hair thought 'glamorous' and favoured by young Turkish women, especially brides and TV presenters. Not what Barbara had expected, (but then, she thought to herself, she hadn't been expecting a girlfriend at all). Gul was staring at her, and their eyes met for a second. In them Barbara sensed hatred, and it made her feel embarrassed and ashamed. She looked away quickly.

'Come on, you're right, let's go,' she shouted over the noise to Mehmet, and they stumbled out through the door.

'Sorry, I . . . we should not have gone there,' Mehmet said as they walked away quickly, 'I know they are there often, I did not think, sorry.'

'It's OK. I just felt a bit embarrassed. It probably wasn't very nice for her, either. Or for poor Osman. Forget it.'

Although it was already late, they sat out on the roof terrace outside Barbara's room when they returned to the hotel. Mehmet brought brandy up from the bar, and they had a pot of 'English' coffee, as he called it. They were both very well aware that it was Barbara's last night, but rushing to bed for a final night of passion just didn't seem to be a priority for either of them. Talking, listening, and just being alone together, alone, was.

A good two hours later, they were standing together at the terrace wall, looking into the streets at the late-night revellers and tourists weaving their way home—or to their hotels. Only then, as they laughed at a quip of Barbara's, did the mood change and suddenly they were kissing, removing clothing, and heading for the bedroom.

In the few hours left of that last night they made love four times. Barbara, having been celibate for so long, was reminded, yet again how much she relished active, adventurous and exciting sex; although nothing felt rushed, both of them taking time—touching and being touched. But still the inevitable morning arrived too quickly.

Just as had happened with Rosalind's departure, it seemed to Barbara that one minute she was having a shower and getting dressed, and the next, she was in Atila's taxi, heading for the airport. She'd managed to 'keep it together' while saying farewell to Mehmet, helped by the presence of Mags, who got up to see her off, and even Osman had been there. But once in the taxi, and despite Atila's kind attempt at 'chirpy' conversation, Barbara's vision blurred, and she cried silently; hot tears rolling down her cheeks.

TWELVE

Oxford: February 1995

Barbara had gone to Henry's funeral the week after she returned from Istanbul. She went with Gareth, and found the whole occasion completely unreal. Barbara had said nothing to Gareth about meeting Rosalind and Mags at the hotel, and at the funeral, they had greeted Barbara simply as one of the many 'wives of academic colleagues' present. No-one would have guessed that she, Rosalind and Mags had been in the same place at the same time only a fortnight previously. But it wasn't at all done in an unfriendly way; just lacking the intimacy of their conversations in Turkey.

The next day, however, Rosalind had phoned Barbara at her office, suggesting they meet, and both of them were relieved to talk 'normally' to one another again. The following Saturday, the three women had met for lunch. 'Oh Lord, I found it ghastly, didn't you?' Mags had linked arms with Barbara as they walked from the car park through to the pub garden by the river, where Rosalind was waiting for them. 'It was so odd, wasn't it? The funeral I mean. We all had our 'Oxford faces' on, didn't we? It was like an extended 'role play' exercise all day for us—'Bereaved widow and friend of same', even though everybody there was perfectly well aware of the nature of our relationship—he was so ancient, poor old Henry.'

That was the first of regular meetings between them. They would have lunch; or spend an afternoon in Woodstock or Burford, browsing the bookshops, and what Mags called the 'twinky shops' that sold expensive gifts and kitchen equipment. Or Barbara would go to supper with them at Rosalind's house in Summertown. The hesitation that Barbara had felt about wanting to remain friends with Mags and Rosalind disappeared within a few weeks; they enjoyed one another's company enormously and Barbara so looked forward to seeing them.

Her relationship with Gareth was coming to an end. They both knew it. In the months after her return from Istanbul, Barbara tried to spend as little time as possible at home with him—a very big reason for her to be thankful for the invitations she received from Rosalind and Mags. She especially valued Rosalind's thoughts and advice about her marriage, and the non-judgemental support she received from both women.

'You have to do what is right for <u>you</u>,' Rosalind had said to her. 'And I know that the trouble with that advice is that most of the time, none of us knows what we want, or what to do for the best. All I can say is that I find, even if at times I don't know what I want, I always know what I <u>don't</u> want, and that's a start. Have you tried writing lists of 'pros' and 'cons'—as regards ending or trying to save your marriage?' Barbara was already a fan of list-making, and 'writing it out of the system'. But other things Rosalind said to her were helping her to reach decisions about her situation. At her house one Friday evening, after dinner, Rosalind had talked about life being 'not a rehearsal', and the importance of at least trying to achieve whatever it is you wish to do—however small the dream, it has to be worth a try. She spoke about a 'sadness' which, she believed, occurred to 'thinking' people once they reached the age of forty-five or so. 'The awful realisation that one has less time left ahead than one has already had—forty-five years up to now, and unlikely to have that many ahead before 'shuffling off'. That's why it becomes imperative—urgent, even, to get on with the important things—to be as happy as it's possible to be for whatever time is left to us.'

Barbara was almost ready. She decided that she would talk to Gareth about separation, and divorce, very soon. But she knew she had to go on a work trip to Azerbaijan in early February, and felt that 'the big conversation' could wait until she returned.

'Barbara? Hello, it's Mags. Sorry to miss you, just wanted to check that you can come on Saturday. Ring us back if you like. But hope to see you about eight—OK? Hope you're all right. Bye.'

It was the first of many messages on Barbara's answerphone. She had enjoyed Azerbaijan because it felt so Turkish—although knew not to say so while she was there, relations between the two countries being historically hostile. Baku, the capital, stank of oil, a 'fact' she'd read in various guidebooks but not really believed until she experienced it for herself. But there were fascinating old parts of the city, and a wonderful, ancient 'Turkish' bathhouse, which she visited twice, feeling very exotic, and very far from home, in the echoing coolness. In the centre of the complex was an indoor fountain, and tables where customers could have refreshments after their baths, served by a charming Azeri couple who ran the place. It was a true oasis among the busy exhaust-fumed streets, and Barbara loved it.

Amongst her post, on her return, were three letters from Mehmet, and an 'At Home' invitation from Rosalind; it was to be a small gathering in the extremely large house in Lonsdale Road in North Oxford where her husband Henry had lived and which Rosalind had inherited on his death. The house had been completely renovated in the last six months, as Rosalind intended to live there with Mags; her 'other house', in Staverton Road, being converted into two large flats, and let out to visiting academics and their families.

Gareth was as sullen as he'd been before she left. Barbara wanted to see Rosalind before she spoke to him about splitting up, and looked forward to the party.

She tore open Mehmet's letters—they were sweetly romantic, as always, although he wrote also of difficulties; he thought it unlikely that the university would allow him to resume his course, which left him vulnerable as far as National Service was concerned. Barbara had spoken to him several times on the phone, when he'd asked, over and over, when she would return to see him again. She had begun to think of going to Istanbul again in January, but knew that once she had started the process of separating from Gareth, she would have a lot of things to sort out at home. She then started wondering if she should wait until she'd visited Mehmet again. And with all the wondering and thinking, time passed without any action being taken at all. It was already the middle of February.

'Going for another threesome with the lesbians tonight?' Gareth threw the words at her as he passed the bathroom, where Barbara was getting ready for the party.

'For fuck's sake, they're NOT lesbians, and even if they were, is there really any need for you to be so nasty about them? But it's not really about them, is it? You've no reason to be angry with them; it's me you're getting at, as usual.'

She came out onto the landing, and called after him as he went down the stairs 'I think it's time we sat down and had a talk, actually . . . Gareth—I think we should talk.' As soon as she spoke, she wondered what on earth she was thinking of, standing there in her dressing gown, mascara brush in hand, due at Rosalind's in less than two hours—hardly the best time for 'the big conversation'. But she'd said it now.

There was no response from Gareth, so she went downstairs and into the lounge. He was sitting at the dining table, hands clasped in front of him. 'Did you hear what . . .' she began.

'Yes. And yes, I think so too.'

'You do? You think we should talk? You're always so scathing about 'talking things out'—that's why you wouldn't go to "Relate" when I suggested it years ago, if you remember?'

'And I still think that—the world's full of "worthies" who think that everything can be put right by talking about 'feelings', emotions. It's crap. What if people don't want to 'open up' and lay all their emotions out for dissection? No, I said it's a good idea for us to talk, now, because I have things to say.'

Gareth then delivered his bombshell—he told her that over the last eight months he had come to the conclusion that he would be happier if he was not married. He'd spent a lot of time working with Giles, a colleague who was in his early sixties and a widower, and as their friendship grew, he had grown increasingly sure that Giles' bookish, rather solitary lifestyle was the sort that would suit him, as well.

Barbara later told Rosalind that she was sure she must have been standing, listening to this, with her mouth open. She was amazed. Gareth had gone on to say that his friend Giles had offered him a room in his house, if he needed somewhere to stay while 'working things out' with Barbara, and he'd accepted; he hoped to move within the month. He ended by saying he hoped they could 'arrange everything' amicably.

Barbara felt as if she'd been 'let off the hook'. After her initial shock at what Gareth was saying to her, she just felt hugely relieved. She'd been expecting a huge row, and that she would be the instigator of it all. Instead, they were able, fairly calmly, to discuss how they would go about the sale of the house, and the 'division and dispersal' of everything in it. Gareth didn't ask her what she was going to do, whether she had any plans. But that was typical of him—setting out what he wanted and leaving it there for everyone else to fall in with or ignore as they chose. She thought it odd that she felt no sadness—it was the end of their marriage after all. But she just felt happy that at last, she could plan a different life for herself, whatever, wherever, and whoever that might involve.

By the time she got to Rosalind's house that night, she felt almost euphoric and couldn't wait to tell her and Mags what had just happened.

THIRTEEN

'Well it seems obvious to me, dear, if it helps you out, of course you must live there.' Rosalind, Barbara, and Mags were sitting in the kitchen, drinking coffee, the morning after the party. Barbara had stayed the night, in one of the many, beautifully-decorated spare bedrooms, after drinking far too much champagne. Rosalind had suggested, on hearing Barbara's story, that she rent the ground floor flat in her old house in Staverton Road. It was available immediately, which meant that the sale of Barbara and Gareth's house wouldn't be held up while she found somewhere else to live.

'You see, it's happened again,' she said to them. 'I've wanted to live in North Oxford for so long, and never thought I'd be able to—and now this. I told you that good things happen to me!'

The next fortnight flew by; Barbara and Gareth closed their joint account, engaged an estate agent, and did all the things necessary in tying up the ends of a relationship—most of which involved huge amounts of documentation and multiple signatures. They went through the contents of their house quite painlessly. As they had not 'bought things together' in the way many couples do—furniture had come from one or other side of the family, and as each of them had lived alone before their marriage, each had their own 'stuff', which made separating it out again easier. They even went out for a couple of meals at the local pub, during this time, something which had been a rare event before. It was all so 'normal', and calm. Gareth had far fewer belongings than Barbara, and moved out at the end of the first week, leaving her to prepare for her own move alone, which she appreciated, as it meant that friends could come and help out without the embarrassment and awkwardness of running into Gareth.

Barbara wrote to Mehmet and told him what had happened, choosing her words carefully so that he wouldn't think that she had suddenly decided she couldn't live without him and had ended her marriage to be with him. She didn't know what she wanted—Rosalind's words came back to her—but she knew she didn't want to be married to Gareth any longer, more than that she didn't know. She was looking forward to having space to herself—and to kitting out her new home; she made lists and doodled plans for furnishing the various rooms in the margins of agendas during tedious meetings at work. Her colleagues, without exception, were pleased for her, and came up with offers of all kinds of help—from packing and removals, to advice on what and what not to dig up and transplant from the garden.

Barbara realised how she had neglected her friends in Oxford since she had married Gareth, and now there was only herself to think about, she started to accept invitations again. She went to the cinema, for walks at the weekends, and joined in inter-office competitions and outings—skittles, ten-pin bowling, pub quizzes. She also returned to sing at folk clubs and sessions, meeting up again with many old friends and getting just as much pleasure from knowing them and their circle as she had always done, 'before'.

'There's always going to be a 'before' and an 'after' when it comes to Gareth, isn't there?' she said to Mags one afternoon when they were putting up blinds in the kitchen of the flat. 'I guess that's inevitable, but it seems odd to keep saying it. I expect as time passes, I'll think of it less in those terms and just get on with life as it is.'

'Sometimes, I find it hard to remember some of the things in my life before I met Rosalind,' Mags replied. 'It's not so much 'before and after', more like that I've had completely different lives. And for all we know, we might, all of us, have several more 'lives' in store for us. We just don't know what will happen. It's a bit frightening, really.'

'Yes, you're right, but it's also exciting—I mean, it's what life is all about, isn't it? Greeting each new day as the start of 'the rest of whatever is going to happen next'.'

Mags told Barbara, that afternoon, about how she'd gone to Oxford straight from school, reading Anthropology, and had met Rosalind—and Henry—in her first term. Rosalind had been her personal tutor, and things just 'fell into place' after they had travelled to Syria together on a field trip. 'We started to do most things together, when we came back from that trip,' she said. 'And then she suggested that I move into her house when I had to get out of my digs—and we've been together, like we are, ever since. Henry was always lovely to me. I think he thought of me as a daughter, really. I know I'm lucky, not having to earn a living or pay rent or having a mortgage and children—responsibilities like that. My father left me enough money to tick by on, but it wouldn't have been enough to buy a house or anything. I'm very aware that I'm fortunate, you know?'

'Did you ever think you would have children, Mags? Or a boyfriend or husband?'

'Oh lord, you sound like some of the Turkish people we met when we were travelling! They simply couldn't understand why a woman of my age was not with her husband and didn't have children.'

'Yes—sorry, you know I didn't mean it like that. I've had that, too, when I was there with Gareth. Several times, a hotel-owner, or even a waiter, having learned that we were 'childless' would say to me, quietly, 'What is problem that you have no children? Is it your husband has problem?' It was hilarious. I'm sure some people would find that kind of thing outrageously rude, but I thought it was funny. I just told them that Gareth had health problems and left it at that. But what about you? You didn't answer my question.'

'Oh, I had a couple of boyfriends when I was in my teens, and a couple when I was first up here. I went on dates in my first year, but, and I know this might sound odd, I just couldn't be bothered with it all. I'm not a virgin, technically, I had very uncomfortable sex, twice, just before I came to Oxford, with a chap I'd known since primary school days. After that, I suppose I just preferred to avoid it.'

'Well, as Rosalind says: 'You must do what's right for you.' And I think you do just that, don't you? I admire both of you for doing so.'

The day before Barbara moved into the flat, a parcel arrived for her, from Istanbul. In it were two beautiful tapestry cushion covers and a card from Mehmet— 'For your new home'. Barbara was touched by his gift, he'd never sent anything before except his letters. That evening, she put the covers into the top of one of the packing cases waiting ready in the garage for the arrival of various friends and their vans and cars in the morning. Then, not having anything else left to do, and because we so often do strange things at such times, she cleaned the kitchen floor; wrote out a list of which keys fitted which doors; and finally went to bed to sleep in the house for the last time.

She woke at six o'clock with that strange feeling of panic, which lasts only seconds, that 'something's happened', before remembering that the 'something' was that today she was moving out, and the panic was replaced by excitement. Mags was the first to arrive, at about eight o'clock, with her friend Vanessa's husband, Anthony, in his large Volvo estate car. 'We've got croissants!' she announced, 'I hope you haven't packed the kettle?' They ate them with coffee, sitting in the bare kitchen, and then packed the 'Fragile and Precious' things (labelled as such in their boxes), into Anthony's car.

'All right then, Shirley?' It was Barbara's colleague, Ed, calling in through the open front door. He'd come with what he called his 'dump truck'—actually a Luton van—but which was used mainly for trips to the dump and to help friends move large items of furniture. Ed had called Barbara 'Shirley' ever since discovering that she had returned to see someone (Mehmet) she met on holiday the year before. On her first day back at work after that last eventful trip to Istanbul, Ed had greeted her with 'Here she is, 'Shirley Valentine'!' Barbara didn't mind in the least, Ed was a good sort and the proof of that was that he was helping her to move.

By lunchtime, the majority of the large furniture and most of the packing cases were at the flat. They took a break and ate delicious 'lunchpacks' from the local Lebanese deli, which another couple of Barbara's colleagues, Anna and Richard, had brought round. There was even a selection of *baklava*, arranged on a tray, which was a gift from Ali, the owner of the deli.

'He asked after you, and when we told him what we were doing today, he got all excited and said he had to send you a moving-in present!' Anna said.

Rosalind had been in the flat since early morning, and she'd stocked the fridge with what she called 'essentials', including two bottles of champagne, which, in Rosalind's mind, were 'essentials' for a moving day!

'It really *is* true', said Mags. 'What you said about things happening to you, isn't it? I've been noticing, since you told us.'

'Maybe it's my dad, looking out for me, or something. I don't know, but I'm very lucky, whatever it is.'

It was nearly six o'clock by the time Barbara and Mags found themselves alone in what had been Gareth and Barbara's house. Everyone else had done their bit and gone home. They did a last hoover, checked and re-checked every room and cupboard, then took the cleaning equipment out to the car.

'That's it, then', Barbara said as she locked the front door for the last time.

'You OK?' Mags asked, her hand on Barbara's arm.

'Absolutely. I never felt that I 'bonded' with this house, if that's the right expression. I had such great hopes for it, being in a lovely village, but it was never 'right'.'

'Maybe it would have been right if you had been with the right person. It's not really the house that's at fault, is it? It's a nice house. Just not right for you, not now, and not with Gareth.'

'Guess so. Come on, I've got to put the keys through the letterbox at the estate agents in Headington. There's an envelope in the glovebox for them. Let's go for a drink at the pub, on the way.'

'Just one, then, don't forget there's champagne in the fridge back at your new home!'

FOURTEEN

March 1995

Contentment. No other word for it. Barbara was sitting on the deep bay windowsill of her flat, looking out at the garden which was lit by early spring sunshine. It was a Saturday morning and she'd now lived there over a month, and still couldn't believe her luck. She'd arranged all of the rooms and had started to plant out different areas of the garden. She loved having no-one to please but herself. She felt a new confidence, even at work.

'Don't laugh,' she'd said to Rosalind one evening, 'But for the first time in my life I don't feel as if someone's always about to tell me off about something!'

'Oh I know exactly what that feels like, dear, but well done —I was about fifty before I got to that point!'

'Really? That's . . . well, I just always thought it was only me who felt like that. Everyone else—at least people around me at work and here in Oxford, appears to know what they're doing—or it seems as if they do!'

'Ooh, no, no, no—most people are in a crisis of confidence for most of their lives, I think.' Rosalind had replied.

Now, as she sat in the window, she thought about Mehmet—he had last phoned her over a week ago, sounding confused and distressed. He'd said that he was going to have to make a decision soon, and that he would probably leave Turkey 'for a while at least', in order to avoid going into the army. Before Barbara could question him further, he'd quickly said he would let her know where he was as soon as he could, and had rung off.

It was one of those strange, almost eerily quiet mornings, Barbara could hear no traffic or even birdsong, the air itself seemed stilled and the light had a peculiar quality. She thought that on such a morning one could almost expect there to be a 'Clap!' and the world would fold up and end. But she shook herself from gazing into the middle-distance and got up to answer the phone.

'Barbara? *Merhaba canim*, are you OK?' She was relieved to hear Mehmet's voice.

'I'm fine, but how are you? Are you all right? I've been worried about you.'

'I'm in Baku—in Azerbaijan. I came here with Şerif, you remember him?'

'Of course, but where are you staying? Is everything all right—you're not in any trouble, are you?'

'Trouble? No, it is fine. I will get a job here and then it will be OK—I will not have to go in the army if I am not in Turkey for a while.'

'Really? How long do you have to stay away?'

'It is three years, but then if I go back I have to pay them and they let me do only about a month in army. I think it is better.'

'Well, yes, it's better than doing the full time, but will you be able to get a job OK?'

'Şerif's brother lives here, I am staying with his family until I get a place. He will get me a job in the casino maybe. Şerif has gone back to Istanbul now.'

'Casino? Can you do that? I guess it's not that different to managing a hotel, is it? What about Ali, is he OK?'

'Yes, my brother will be fine, I will send money to the family he is with. They are good people, they will look after him.'

'Listen, Mehmet, I know people in Baku, I was there for work a while ago, remember? I will give you the address of the office and you must go and see them, OK?'

'I do not have pen now—do not worry, you can give me address another time. I will send you a letter with address for me.'

Then he was gone, leaving Barbara alone, still holding the telephone, in the strange silence she'd noticed before his call.

The following Monday, Barbara went into work early, and typed out a fax to the Baku office, telling them that a friend of hers was in Baku, and to expect him to call in. She had 'special responsibility' for Eastern Europe in her work, the Caucasus region in particular, and it was not beyond the realms of possibility that she, too, would be back in Azerbaijan before too long. With this in mind, she arranged to see the organisation's Regional Director that afternoon.

On Barbara's visit to Azerbaijan, she had learned a great deal about the country's ongoing conflict with Armenia—she had met many people forced to leave their homes in the disputed territories. The same thing had happened to Armenian families who found themselves 'in the wrong place'. Barbara's organisation was working in refugee camps hastily erected in both countries, and now that it was beginning to look like some tentative attempts at peace negotiations were to take place, there was more support to small organisations working with 'vulnerable groups'—people with disabilities, women, and children left in charge of families through the parent-robbing atrocity of war.

As it turned out, she discovered at her meeting, Barbara was about to be asked to return to Azerbaijan for a week, to assist the groups she had worked with earlier in the year in the preparation of funding proposals for the coming financial year. She felt relieved that she didn't have to persuade the Director to send her back there immediately— she had been slightly worried that she would not be able to hide her 'ulterior motive'. When she left work that evening, she went straight round to see Mags and Rosalind, knowing they were always interested and concerned for Mehmet.

'Things working out the way they should for you again,' said Mags, on hearing that Barbara was to set off for Baku the following Saturday.

'You do think that he is all right, dear, from what he said on the phone?' Rosalind asked.

'I think so, but it's so hard to tell. And he wasn't on the phone for long. Oh hell—I've just thought—how am I to let him know I'm going to be in Baku? He just said he'd write to me with his address. That could take weeks!'

'Didn't you say you'd told him about the office address? You'll just have to hope he contacts them.' Said Mags.

'Or you might have to spend a few nights doing the rounds of all the casinos in Baku!' Rosalind added, quite seriously. 'I wonder if there are many there? With all the new American oil companies moving in, I wouldn't be surprised.'

When Barbara got home she wandered around the flat, then out into the garden, smoking too many cigarettes and fretting about how she was to contact Mehmet. *'Fat lot of use it'll be—me in the same city and him not knowing it!'* she thought to herself. At two o'clock in the morning she was sitting up in bed with a notepad, scribbling down all the different people she'd met with Mehmet in Istanbul, along with various people and places he'd mentioned to her.

'Come on, there must be some way of finding out where he's living,' she thought. *'I'm a researcher, this is 'do-able'.'*

She ruled out the University—there was unlikely to be any record of him there other than that he was no longer one of their students. Then she remembered what he'd said on the phone—he was staying with Şerif's brother's family in Baku. Şerif—the brother of Gul, the poor girl so in love with Mehmet. In her mind, she took herself back to her last night in Istanbul—Bar Oxygen and seeing Gul with her friends. *'Of course—Osman knows her, so will probably know the family too! I'm sure he'd find out for me, if he can.'* And with this small breakthrough, she settled down to sleep, determined to contact The Meydan the next day and try to reach Osman.

It was all too easy.

Barbara had sent a fax to the hotel the next day, asking if 'Mr Osman' was working that day and if so, to please reply confirming that he would be able to speak on the phone to her at 2pm, their time. Not only was Osman there, but he must have been right next to the fax machine, for the reply came straight back from him.

She went home at lunchtime and called the hotel. Osman sounded so excited to hear her, he kept saying:

'You call *me* from England!' It was a few moments before Barbara could get him to stop interrupting her and she was able to ask if he could find out Mehmet's address—or even better, a telephone number in Baku.

'No problem,' he said.

'Shall I call you tomorrow, will that give you enough time to get it?'

'No, it is not necessary, I have it. I have telephone number for Mehmet.'

'Oh that's great, Osman, I am going there, so I want to meet him, you see.'

'He will be happy to see you. He is missing you. I am missing you too.'

'Thank you, Osman, you are always very nice to me. I hope to see you again in Istanbul one day.'

As he told her the number, repeating it twice, and she was writing it down, a sudden thought occurred to her—'Osman, Mehmet is staying with Şerif's brother, yes?'

'That is right, he lives in Baku.'

'So he is Gul's brother as well?'

'Yes, of course.'

'Um . . . do you think it is OK for me to call the house? Will it be awkward—you know, difficult, for Mehmet?'

'I don't know this. Maybe. I can call him and ask him to call you, maybe?'

'Osman, you are a genius! Would you do that for me? Thank you so much. Ask him to call me one evening this week, before Friday, OK? I am going to Baku on Saturday. Thanks again, very much.'

FIFTEEN

Baku, Azerbaijan
April 1995

Mehmet had called Barbara—but not until the Thursday evening before she left, causing her a few sleepless nights until she heard from him. He had been surprised to get a message that Osman had phoned, and when he spoke to him and learned that Barbara would be in Baku the very next weekend, he couldn't believe it.

'You are coming to see me? But I am OK, you do not have to come because you are worried about me.'

'I'm not coming because you're there, love, I would be coming to Baku anyway—for my job. It's just very fortunate that you are there as well!'

He arranged with her to meet at 11am on Sunday, the day after her arrival, at the café in the Turkish bathhouse she'd visited on her previous trip. But Mehmet being Mehmet, he was at the 'Arrivals' gate, holding a bunch of flowers, when Barbara walked through into the airport concourse late on Saturday night. She was very surprised to see him, and a little taken aback—he had lost weight, and looked older, worried. They clung together, not saying anything, for what seemed a long time.

'This is a bit *deja vu*, isn't it? Like when I arrived in Istanbul?'

'I do not believe it that you are here. It is like a dream.'

'I wouldn't be surprised if you have a cousin here, too, with a taxi waiting.'

'No, I do not have a friend with taxi tonight. But here is better than Istanbul airport—there is café open if you want coffee?'

'Oh marvellous—yes please.' She touched his cheek 'It's so good to see you again, love. Are you OK?'

'Yes, I will tell you it all later, tomorrow. Tonight I get you coffee and then get taxi to the place you are staying—you have address?'

'Yes, of course, it's the same apartment I stayed at last time. It's not far from the office.'

They talked until the waiter started to wipe tables and put chairs on top of tables—obviously about to close up for the night. Mehmet went outside and negotiated the taxi fare to the apartment. When they arrived, he had the taxi wait outside while he carried Barbara's bag up to the door, making sure she was safely through the door before leaving her, kissing her on top of her head before he went. As so often before, she felt a kind of confused detachment from him, as if they had never been intimate.

Barbara found the apartment stocked with tea, coffee and milk, and her colleagues had even left some bread rolls, pastries, chocolate and a bottle of wine, with a note saying 'See you soon, we are happy you are here again!' She made some tea, unpacked a few things, and went to bed. Laying there listening to the sounds of the street outside, she drifted off to sleep.

Next day was beautifully sunny, but a little too hot for Barbara's liking—being in a busy city offered little respite from the heat, and Baku's pervasive smell of oil was ever-present. So Barbara was glad that she was meeting Mehmet at the bath house café—it was so cool in there. She left early, so that she would have some time there before he arrived, to renew her friendship with the nice couple who ran the café.

They were pleased to see her, and 'of course' remembered her, they said, insisting that she take tea with them, scurrying around with little trays, glasses, sweet biscuits, and tiny dishes of jam. When Mehmet arrived, the three of them were chatting. He greeted the couple formally, and sat opposite Barbara, having greeted her, she thought, pretty formally, too. The man and his wife then left them and went back to the kitchen.

'You seem very . . . is it 'at home' you say?' Mehmet smiled at her.

'Yes, I think that's what you mean. I met them last time I was here. They're very nice.'

A young man came to their table with fresh tea.

As Mehmet stirred sugar lumps into his tea, and fiddled with the plate of biscuits, Barbara noticed that he was not looking at her. He seemed nervous, distracted.

'Mehmet, what's wrong, love?' she asked him, putting her hand on his arm.

He looked up and met her eyes, briefly, before looking down again. Then he pushed back his chair and took out his cigarettes, sighing deeply before lighting one.

'Many things have happened.' He said.

'Look, you're worrying me, just tell me what's wrong, enough of this enigmatic stuff, please.'

Mehmet turned to her, looking at her hands on the table. He covered them with his own.

'I am ashamed of what has happened. But I cannot see my way now . . .'

'What are you talking about? What has . . .'

'Please,' He cut her short. 'Let me tell you what I have to and then you will know it all. You know about before you were with me in Istanbul. There was a problem with Şerif's sister, Gul?'

'She was your girlfriend when you were at college, yes. And you didn't tell her I was coming to see you. And there was that awkward night in that club when we saw her, yes. All I know is that she was in love with you but you didn't feel the same way. Even Şerif told me that. But what has that to do with . . .' Mehmet raised his hand and continued.

'After you went home, last summer, she was coming to the hotel. All the time, every day. She wanted to go out with me with our friends again. Osman tried to talk to her, and Şerif. In the end, in November, I agree to go to the wedding of our friends in Bursa together. But there were many of us going, it was not like just a couple.' He paused and lit another cigarette, although he hadn't smoked his first one, it had burned out in the ashtray.

'I am hurting to say this to you,' he said, looking over the top of Barbara's head at the sunlit windows.

'We slept together the night we stayed in Bursa. I had too much alcohol, but it is my fault, not the drinking.'

'Mehmet, stop love, just stop. I think you're forgetting that I was a married woman when we first got together. OK, I know that I wasn't having sex with Gareth, but if I had have been in a 'normal' marriage, I probably would have continued to have sex with my husband once I went home. Our situations—living in different countries—well, that doesn't exactly make it easy to be totally 'committed' to one another, does it. And after what you told me about Gul, I guess I shouldn't have been surprised that you had a girlfriend in Istanbul. So it's not really a 'big deal', is it?'

Barbara looked at him and was shocked to see that his eyes were filled with tears. She felt hot and suddenly tearful herself.

'Well, is it?'

'She is going to have a baby. My baby,' he said, and looked into her eyes for the first time.

'Oh for fuck's sake! You idiot! Why didn't you use condoms? Don't tell me, you were drunk. When is the baby due—August?'

She was angry with him for being stupid; for getting into a mess that would affect what he did with the rest of his life. More that, than feeling hurt that he'd got another woman pregnant.

'So what are you going to do?' she asked him, coolly.

'It was when she told me, and she told her family, then they help me get out of Turkey and come here. So I don't go in the army. They help me because I am father of the child. No other reason.'

'And you couldn't see another way of getting out of it? Christ—you didn't PLAN it, did you?'

'Of course I did not do that! I would not do that, I am not a bad person who can do that sort of thing!'

'OK, OK,' She could tell by his reaction to her question that it wouldn't have occurred to him to sacrifice his future like that.

'I told you I am ashamed. I know you will be angry with me and upset. I have hurt you and I do not want this to happen.' He took her hand again, but Barbara moved it away.

'What *is* going to happen, then? Are you going to marry her?'

'It is what she wants, of course. And her family—except Şerif—think that will happen, but . . .'

'What do you mean 'except Şerif'?'

'Şerif knows me as a friend. He knows that it is not what I want. He knows I do not love his sister. He thinks it would be wrong to marry. He also thinks that she might have planned to trap me like this—by having a baby. But she knows I do not love her or want to be married with child.'

'You should have thought of that before getting her pregnant—it takes two to make a baby, you know?' Barbara hated herself for being so harsh with him, but just couldn't help it. She was confused and angry. She brushed his arm. 'I'm sorry, I didn't mean to be horrible to you. Look, I'd like to have some time on my own now, OK? I think I'll go back to the apartment.'

She motioned to the waiter for the bill, but the man who ran the café called out to her 'No, no madam—it is for you, you do not pay on first day back here!'

Barbara thanked him and promised to call again later in the week. Then she and Mehmet went out into the lunchtime heat and dust, which hit them so noticeably after the cool café.

SIXTEEN

They parted, rather awkwardly, outside the café, not seeming to have anything more to say to one another at that point. Mehmet asked if Barbara wanted to see him again while she was there, and she told him not to be so daft, that of course she would see him, and asked him to call at the apartment the following Tuesday evening. Then she left him, and set off in the direction of the apartment. Mehmet walked towards the main square.

All Barbara could think, as she walked, was that she was now facing a week working in Baku, with all this stuff 'dumped' on her on the first morning of what she had hoped would be a happy time. She felt very far from home and the comforts of Oxford, her flat, and her friends. A car blared its horn and startled her. Realising she'd already walked past the road leading to the apartment, she changed her mind about going there and instead, crossed the road and headed for the ancient part of the city. She had spent some time there on her last trip, and enjoyed the old buildings and the little shops, cafés and museums housed in them. She always liked the feeling of Sundays in non-Christian countries; the bustling, 'day out with the family' atmosphere, when at home few shops would be open, and most families stayed firmly indoors around the TV, or sleeping off their Sunday lunch.

The lanes of the old city were quiet; Barbara was the only person walking around, it seemed. The restaurants and cafés were serving lunch in their little inner courtyards and she could hear happy chatter and laughter; occasionally a child's voice, raised in complaint, and a mother's soothing words in response. Outside many of the shops and cafés stood the men who worked in them, all greeted her in heavily-accented English: 'Hello, hello, madam! Lady—you come to look? For tea? For meal? We are happy to welcome you.' Several times, Barbara had to stop herself answering in Turkish, as she would have done in Istanbul—Mehmet had taught her how to say 'I am not a tourist' and other useful phrases useful for dealing politely with over-insistent shopkeepers. But she knew no Azeri apart from basic greet-ings, 'please' and 'thank you', picked up on her first trip, so although it seemed so much like Turkey, she had to play the tourist in Baku, and she found herself enjoying the experience.

Outside a small 'gift boutique' she selected a few postcards from the rack, paid the man inside, and then went back to a café fronted by three particularly charming waiters who were delighted to hear that she wanted to enter and have tea. They fussed over her table setting, in a quiet corner of the courtyard, away from the people eating lunch, next to a gently babbling water fountain in the centre of a tiled pool, where large goldfish swam lazily.

'*Well*,' she wrote to Rosalind and Mags, '*this is not going to be the kind of week I thought it was to be.*' She wrote briefly and cryptically that she'd received 'news' from Mehmet that was going to take some getting used to, but that she was OK, there was no need to worry about her, and she would see them soon to explain further. As she addressed the card, she felt desperately homesick.

When she returned to the apartment, she found a note addressed to her had been pushed through the letterbox. It was from Samira and Ashan, her colleagues from the Baku office, inviting her to join them at the *Dostlar* ('Friends') Restaurant that evening for dinner at seven pm. Barbara was so pleased that they had invited her out, she enjoyed their company, and was relieved that she would not be spending the evening alone in the apartment, dwelling on her thoughts about Mehmet. She had a shower and spent a while sitting on the balcony wearing a beautiful silk bathrobe that had been hanging on the back of the bedroom door—left for her by her thoughtful colleagues, she suspected. She wrote in her travel journal about where she had been that morning, and described the old city streets and the café she'd been to. *'It all sounds so 'normal', as if it's just another trip I'm writing up,'* she thought as she read over what she'd written. *'Aye, well, 'keep calm and carry on!''* she thought, quoting the famous Second World War poster. *'Can't do much else at the moment!'*

At six-fifteen she set out to walk to the restaurant in Fountain Square. It was cooler now, and the streets were busy with smartly-dressed people out walking; pausing to greet friends at café tables; 'seeing and being seen'. Barbara smiled as she thought it was just like the *'passeggiata'* one sees taking place in Italian cities in the early evening. As she entered the Square at one side, she stopped dead. Right in front, but with his back to her, was Mehmet, sitting at a table outside one of the many bar/cafés, with an older man and a young boy. She turned and walked along the far side, right around the edge of the square instead of going straight to the restaurant, which was quite close to where Mehmet was sitting. She didn't know why she felt so unsettled by seeing him unexpectedly, but by the time she met her friends at the restaurant she was flushed and felt apprehensive. Although it was a very pleasant evening with good food, wine and conversation, Barbara remained distracted. They ate at a table outside the restaurant, and she had to fight the temptation, to look around, constantly, scanning the crowds, in case she spotted Mehmet again. As the meal drew to a close, her friends ordered a taxi for themselves, and insisted they would drop Barbara at the apartment on their way home. She would have enjoyed the walk, and some time alone, but gave in gracefully. Although she was quite close to Samira, and had talked with her about their personal lives and relationships during her last visit, she had been circumspect when Samira asked her about Mehmet.

'Your friend you told us was in Baku—he did not come to the office. Is he still here?'

'He, er . . . I think so, I don't really know at the moment,' Barbara had replied, grateful that the chatter around the table that evening had prevented her from discussing it further, and in hindsight, she thought it was better that way, for now.

There was again a note waiting for her at the apartment, this time from Mehmet: '*I am sorry for today. If you do not want to meet again I will understand this. I will come Tuesday 19:00 to apartment and if you do not want me do not open door. I will go away. Sorry. Mehmet*'

Barbara felt more frustrated with him than ever, when she read this. She realised that she was actually 'moving on', in her mind, even since that morning. Already, she was thinking if there was anything she could do to help Mehmet in his difficult situation; she wanted to know more about what the girl's family had planned for her—and for him, for that matter. Mulling it all over, she fell asleep on the huge, lumpy settee in the lounge, and woke, uncomfortable and cold, at three o'clock, when made herself some tea and took herself off to bed for what was left of the night.

SEVENTEEN

Fortunately, none of Barbara's work that week would take her very far from Baku, so she would be back at the apartment every night. She spent most of Tuesday at a community advice centre in the dreadfully polluted town of Sumgayit, known as 'the chemical town' due to its having been the hub of the region's petro-chemical industry in Soviet times. With the break up of the Soviet Union, the factories fell into disrepair; unemployment soared; and local people looted the derelict buildings for whatever they could use. Huge vats of chlorine stood unguarded on these premises, and Barbara was horrified to learn that many women and children had suffered burns to their skin from accidental spills when fetching the awful stuff in buckets to sell at local markets. In the absence of affordable detergents, women had taken to adding chlorine to the water for household washing and cleaning.

It had been a long and upsetting day, but as usual on these trips, Barbara was gratified that the work her organisation was funding was making a positive difference to the lives of so many families. When she got back to her temporary 'home' in Baku, she had a long shower, dried her hair, and again wearing the silk robe, poured herself a glass of the wine Samira and Ashan had left for her and took it onto the balcony. She sat there and smoked a cigarette, watching the comings and goings of people in the street below. She lost herself in her thoughts about all kinds of people and things—the early evening sunshine warming her skin. As she stared into space, she realised that the man about to cross the road opposite her was Mehmet, coming to see her, as agreed, at 7pm. As she jumped up to go inside and fling on some clothes, her foot caught the small balcony table and sent her wine glass flying; it smashed on the floor and soaked the hem of the robe in red wine.

'Oh Jesus CHRIST!' she shouted out loud, startling an elderly woman on the next balcony who was hanging out washing. Barbara went to the kitchen to fetch kitchen roll, a cloth, or even tissues to clear up the mess. On her way past the front door, the doorbell rang—Mehmet had arrived. So departed any thoughts she may have had of appearing calm, cool and collected when she saw him that evening. When she opened the door, she was wearing a wine-stained bath robe, holding a grubby cloth in one hand, and the broken stem of a wine glass in the other!

'What has happened? Are you OK? Here, give me that,' Mehmet took the broken glass from her. 'But you are bleeding, what happened?'

'No, it's only wine,' Barbara said. 'I knocked the glass over on the balcony.'

'Yes, but your foot it is bleeding, I think you cut it.'

She looked down and groaned—there was blood on the carpet, a trail of marks across to the kitchen and back, she hadn't noticed that she'd cut the top of her foot on the broken glass.

'Come,' Mehmet said to her, tossing onto the coffee table the leather shoulder bag and a bunch of flowers he'd been holding. 'Sit down, I will look—you should wash it. I will get water, you stay there.' He helped her to sit on the settee, her injured foot on the coffee table.

He went to the kitchen and returned with a small bowl of water and a towel. Barbara told him that her medical kit was in a bag on the bed, from which he fetched antiseptic and dressings.

As he let the water run over her foot, and gently bathed the several small cuts there, Barbara started to cry. 'I'm sorry, love, I'm OK, really, I didn't even feel anything, honestly, I'm all right. I'm sorry, this is so stupid,' she garbled.

'It will be all right, there is no glass in your foot,' he said. 'You were lucky. If you had bad cut and you here on your own it would not be good.'

'Oh I'm always lucky, I've told you that, before,' Barbara snivelled into a tissue, as Mehmet carefully tied a lint dressing around her foot. 'But look what I've done—the carpet is a mess, and this—'she dabbed at the wine stains on her robe.

'Don't worry, I will make tea and you will drink it and I can clean this—no, you stay there,' he said, as she attempted to rise from the settee. While he was in the kitchen, Barbara noticed the flowers for the first time. She felt her eyes well up again. 'You brought me flowers again,' she called to him.

'Of course I bring you flowers, I should bring you much more but I did not know if . . .' he called back, his words trailing off mid-sentence.

'I wouldn't have let you come over to see me this evening and not answer the door, you know? I've been thinking about you, and what you've told me, and all I want to do is to see if there's anything I can do to help—what is going to happen, once Gul's had the baby?'

Mehmet came back into the lounge, strode over to her, bent down and took her hands in his, kissing them and holding them to his forehead 'You are an amazing woman,' he told her. 'I am afraid, coming here, that I will not see you again and now you say 'can you help me?'. About the baby and family I will tell you later. Drink your tea while I clean up.' He picked up the flowers, returned to the kitchen and came back with a small tray, on which was a mug of tea and a carton of milk from the fridge. He had put the flowers in water in the steel pot that held kitchen utensils. He put the tray on the table and pulled a sheepish expression, making Barbara laugh. 'Not very elegant, I'm sorry. I did not see a jug for milk or flowers!'

As she drank her tea, Mehmet picked up the broken glass on the balcony and cleaned up the wine spilt there. Then he started on the blood-stained carpet, which wasn't too bad a job, as it was quite old and a dirty-brown colour to start with.

Outside, the light was fading. Barbara looked at her watch and was surprised to find that Mehmet had been there over an hour already.

'Mehmet—what did you want to do tonight? I mean, have you eaten? We should go out for some food before it gets much later—if you want to.'

'I did not think about eating. But yes, we can go—I know a nice small place just near. I get taxi for us downstairs.'

'Sure, I'm fine, it's not bad at all, love, and I'd like to walk—I'd like some fresh air. We can get a taxi back, maybe? I'll go and get dressed. Oh—I'd forgotten about this—I've ruined this bath robe and it's not mine, it was here when I arrived—it might be Samira's.'

'Give it to me and I will put it in water it will help get the wine out,' Mehmet said, automatically putting his hand out as if to take it from her. They looked at each other; suddenly feeling embarrassed. Barbara got up from the settee and went towards the bedroom. 'I'll bring it out when I've got dressed, won't be a minute,' she said quickly, to hide her confusion.

'This is ridiculous,' she thought as she dressed. *'Why is it that each time we meet it's as if we've never slept together? I feel like a wretched fumbling teenager!'* Once she was ready, she realised how much better she felt, now that Mehmet was here, after the anxiousness she had felt in anticipation of his arrival.

Mehmet had filled the kitchen sink with water and as he took the robe from Barbara, they smiled at each other. 'That'll be OK in the water until we get back,' she said. 'At least there's no chlorine added to this wash!' And as they walked to the restaurant—a little Turkish bistro place—Barbara told him about her day in Sumgayit and the women selling the chlorine.

EIGHTEEN

'I thought you would like it here,' Mehmet said when they had ordered. 'It is like in Istanbul?'

'Yes, you're right, but then I think the whole of Baku is like being in Istanbul. It the same 'feel' to it, somehow.' They chatted as they ate their meal, reminiscing about their time in Istanbul; about the places they had been and about people they had been with—about Rosalind and Mags. Afterwards, they moved to a small raised 'kosk' area, to sit on the cushioned divans for brandy and cigarettes.

Barbara took a deep breath. 'So tell me, what's going to happen about Gul and the baby? She's back in Istanbul now?'

'Yes,' Mehmet paused and lit a cigarette. 'She wants to have the baby there, with her mother and her aunts with her. But I cannot go back to Turkey, you know, for three years now, because of the army thing. So she is talking about coming to live with her brother's family— well, also with me, here in Baku, when baby is born.'

'And she expects to get married?'

Mehmet sighed and leant back against the cushions. 'She does. Her family does.'

'Except Şerif, you said.'

'Yes, except Şerif. He advises me to 'keep it off', is that right? Not to marry for as long a time as I can. To see what happens when we are here after the baby is born.'

'I think he means 'to stall'—to put it off as long as you can?'

'Yes, that's right.'

'It's going to be difficult for you, love, living with the family while you're here, isn't it?'

'That is why I will find somewhere to live, once I have a job, not with her brother.'

'I saw you in Fountain Square on Sunday night, by the way. You were sitting with a man and a young boy.'

'That was Nurettin, Gul's brother and also brother of Şerif, of course. The boy is his son, Tahir.'

'I thought it might be him,' she said. 'And what does Nurettin think about it all?'

'He thinks we will be married and live here when Gul comes here with the baby. Oh, I do not know what to think or do about any of it any more!' Mehmet leant forward, his face in his hands. Then he ran his hands up and over his hair. Barbara thought how lovely he looked. She remembered Rosalind calling him 'a dish', and smiled to herself.

'They are talking to me about some plans,' he continued. 'Then I am thinking about other plans, and Şerif talks to me about not getting married unless I love his sister. My head feels like exploding. And now you are here and I wish it was just you and me and we were in Turkey and none of this was happening.'

Barbara took his hand. 'I know, love, but it is how it is, and wishing it otherwise isn't going to make it so. All you can do is decide what's the best way for you to deal with it, now that it has happened. Can you trust Şerif? I mean, if you can talk to him honestly, even just on the phone, that will help you—and if he comes here to visit his brother, at least you will have a friend here sometimes.'

'I feel ashamed that I can be here—hiding from going in the army, because of her family, but it all happened so fast, Şerif was coming here and suggested that I come with him.'

'It makes you "owe" them, you mean? Yes, I can understand how you feel. What if you were to go somewhere else, on your own? If you could get a job and somewhere to live—you could still stay out of Turkey for three years, couldn't you?'

'I started to think of that when I was in Istanbul. But like I said to you, this all happens and it seemed . . . an easy way. No, that is not really how I thought . . . I hate myself if I think that. I feel so bad about it seeming that way. If I knew someone who did what I have done, I would think they were a bad person.'

'Mehmet, don't give yourself a hard time about this. If you beat yourself up about it now, how are you going to cope later on, when you are having to live and work here on your own? You will make yourself so miserable and unhappy and then you won't be able to sort yourself out at all. And I will be so worried about you. You're NOT a bad person, you've just been a bit stupid and have to deal with the consequences of that. I will help you if I can, I don't know how, but you know I can 'be there' for you, don't you?'

'You are so clever, Barbara. You can see what is true. You make me feel more calm when you talk to me.'

'I'm not that clever,' she said. 'It's called 'cutting through the crap', and that's something I am good at! Shall we go now? It's getting late.'

Mehmet stayed at the apartment that night. They had gone to bed, simply and lovingly holding one another until they slept. They had not made love, and slept until Barbara's alarm clock woke them at seven-thirty. Barbara found herself thinking how 'natural' it felt, as they got up and prepared for the day, making coffee and just being together. Mehmet left an hour later, holding her close and kissing the top of her head before they parted at the door. They arranged to meet that night, at the restaurant they'd been to the previous evening, at seven.

Once he had left, Barbara made herself an instant coffee and sat on the tiny balcony, smoking a cigarette, until her taxi to the office arrived. She had a busy day in the office, writing up the visits she'd made so far, and running over funding proposals that she was to take back with her to Oxford. She told Samira about the spilt wine and apologised for ruining the beautiful robe, but her friend said that the robe was for Barbara, a gift, and she was sorry if it was stained but that she would get her another. Barbara never ceased to be moved by the generosity of the people she worked with on her travels, but she persuaded Samira that when she'd rinsed out the robe that morning, the stain was hardly noticeable, and was sure to come out completely with a proper wash.

Barbara still felt a little awkward in not telling Samira about meeting up with Mehmet. Several times she nearly did, but somehow it didn't feel right. She feared that her friends and colleagues in Baku would think less of her, would not respect her, if they knew. This was probably completely untrue, but it stopped her from confiding in anyone about the increasingly-difficult situation she found herself in—regarding her relationship with Mehmet. She thought a lot about Rosalind and how much she wanted to talk to her about it all. But it was already Wednesday and she was due to leave on Friday evening. She knew that one of the first things she would do, on her arrival home, was to go and see Rosalind and Mags, and she looked forward to hearing what they made of it all.

'Are you sure about the airport on Friday?' Mehmet took Barbara's hand across the table, They were sitting outside the restaurant where they'd just eaten.

'Yes, very sure, love. I would rather you weren't there, I'll worry about you even more if you're with me just before I leave. And Ashan will come with me, I'll be fine.'

'I had a call from Şerif today—he knows you are here and he wants me to ask you something.'

'Şerif? What does he want to ask me? Is he still in Istanbul?'

'Yes, but he is going to be in London—maybe in a few months, and he wants to know if he can call you.'

'What's he going to London for?'

'He has a friend who is living there, the family has a restaurant. Şerif is lucky—he has visa to go to visit them. He said he would like to see you as well, if you do not mind. Maybe he could go to Oxford.'

'That's a bit of a surprise, I didn't think he'd be keen to see me, but yes, you can give him my number and then he can call me when he's in London, OK?'

'OK, I will do that. Thank you, You will ask him to Oxford to see you?'

'Oh, I don't know, I could go to London to see him, but I don't like going up there much. I'll see what he wants to do when he calls me. How did he manage to get a visa? I wish you were able to get one—then you could be in England for your 'three years out' couldn't you?'

'His friend has an uncle who is a politician in Turkey—he arranged it. It is very hard to get visa for UK. I wish it was possible for me, too.'

'Maybe it will be, one day, none of us knows what the future will bring, love.'

'That is true, but I feel that my future is bringing me things I do not want. I do not know how to cope with what I think is going to be my future.'

'Come on, how is it you say that—'Hay-di'? Don't get 'down' about it—we just have to see what happens, and what to do for the best. But for now, well, you know I have to go out tomorrow night again with Samira and the others from work, so tonight's our last night together for a while. Let's try and just enjoy each other's company, OK?'

'I always enjoy your company, *canim*,' Mehmet replied, managing a smile, and he turned to signal the waiter for their bill.

They slept together again that night, but again, had not made love. Barbara hadn't felt awkward about it, and she was sure that Mehmet hadn't, either. It was as if they didn't need to, somehow. She knew their relationship was changing, but whether temporarily or permanently she was unsure.

'I never thought I'd say this,' Barbara had said to Ashan at the Departure Gate, 'but I think I'm getting just a little bit tired of airports and travelling!'

Now, as she waited for take-off, she thought about why she felt like this, and decided that it was something to do with looking forward to going home to her flat, and to having a more contented home life to return to. As the plane taxied out onto the runway and the cabin lights dimmed, she rested her forehead on the window, looking out at the lights of the airport and the other planes, all lined up; all of them, she thought, about to take other people to other places. Maybe on every plane there was someone—more than one, even—feeling as confused and 'fragmented' as she felt herself. She closed her eyes and leant her head back as the plane took off. Below her, she may have been surprised to know, Mehmet stood by the airport's perimeter fence. He watched her plane leave, watched while it circled and until he could see it no longer. He wiped his hand over his eyes and walked back to the taxi rank.

NINETEEN

Oxford, May 1995

'Oh I do love May Morning, but it's knackering!' Barbara laughed as she flopped into one of Rosalind's big, plumpy sofas.

'I still think it's a bit 'off' that they've moved the Bank Holiday this year,' said Rosalind. 'It's all very well commemorating VE Day, but they could have let us have two holidays, I think!'

'Aye well, I don't really mind taking leave,' Barbara replied. 'I tried, once, to do May Morning and then go into work—not a good idea! In fact, I've taken the whole week off this year and I'm really looking forward to the break.'

'Well, it seems that for you it's an all-day event!' laughed Mags. 'We've been down to the bridge a few times in the past, but meeting all your musician friends and having breakfast and everything—it's been a different thing entirely!'

Rosalind and Mags had joined Barbara on Magdalen Bridge to hear the choristers sing at six o'clock, and had then been introduced to some of her 'folkie' friends who were playing or performing with the various Morris dancing sides throughout the rest of the day in and around the city centre. After following the Morris dancers along The High and into Broad Street, they went for the traditional Buck's-Fizz-and-croissants-breakfast at The Oxford Union. While they were there, watching the dancing in the garden, a good-looking man, who spoke with a soft Irish accent, came over and greeted Rosalind. Barbara realised that she had seen him before, at folk sessions in various pubs around Oxford. He played guitar and whistle, and sometimes also sang.

'Surely you two know one another?' Rosalind was saying. 'Barbara, have you met Sean Donahue?'

The man stepped forward, offering Barbara his hand. 'I've seen you at sessions, I like the songs you sing.' Barbara felt slightly embarrassed. 'Oh, I er . . . thank you. I'm Barbara Anderson. Yes, I've seen you— heard you I mean, heard you play, too, of course, yes.' She cringed inside at her burbling gabble.

She looked up and saw Mags *wink* at her, something she'd certainly not done before and which served only to add to Barbara's confusion and embarrassment.

'Well, I'm Sean, pleased to meet you properly,' said Sean, shaking her hand. 'I was one of Rosalind's students, as an under-grad.'

'Oh, an anthropologist? I did anthropology too—but only at the Poly.' Barbara said.

'What do you mean "only"?' Sean said to her, still holding her hand. 'You mustn't say that,' I don't hold with all that 'Fools on the Hill' name-calling nonsense some of the University students come out with.'

'I'm glad to hear it!' said Rosalind, spreading her arms to gather and shepherd them all towards the bar. 'I'm in need of some coffee— shall we go in?'

Barbara wasn't sure how he managed it, but Sean had turned so that he was next to her, managing to place her hand through his arm, his other hand on top of hers. So it was that they followed Rosalind and Mags, into the Union building. As they stood in the queue for coffee, all of them nodding at and greeting those they knew in the jostling crowd, Barbara's attention was drawn to someone moving quickly along the far side of the bar, trying to get to the door. It was Gareth. He kept his head down, his eyes averted, but it was obvious that he had seen them. Barbara looked across at Rosalind, who had also noticed him. She mouthed his name silently at her. Rosalind raised her eyebrows and then shook her head. 'Come on Barbara, there are some people leaving just over there, that small table—you and Sean go and nab it for us.'

They pushed their way through and got to the table just as the previous occupants were leaving.

'You OK? Was that someone you know?' Sean said to her when they were seated.

'No, I mean, yes, I'm fine, it's just that . . . I've just seen my ex-husband.'

'He didn't seem to want to hang around.'

'You can say that again! I'm very surprised he's here, when we were together I always came to May Morning on my own. He said he wasn't interested. Mind you, that could be said of most of the things I was interested in!'

'You said "ex-husband"—can I be rude and ask when you split?'

'It was early this year, February/March time.'

'Painful?'

'No, not at all, actually. What's the cliché— 'Should have done it years ago'?

'OK—just wondered, sorry.' He 'mugged' a smile at her.

'It's fine, really, you don't have to apologise.'

Rosalind arrived with a tray of coffee. Barbara excused herself and went out to the Ladies loo. Inside, drying her hands, was Mags.

'What on earth was that about—winking at me out there?'

'Me? Oh well, you know, he's as much of 'a dish', as Rosalind would say, as your Mehmet, isn't he? And he seems very keen.'

'Mags! For goodness sake! We've only just met and I . . .'

'Not true—you've seen each other at the music sessions haven't you? So you've interests in common, too.'

'Now stop it, don't be silly. I've far too much going on in my life at the moment to think about starting new relationships, thank you!'

'You don't have to 'have a relationship' with him, do you? It would just be nice to have someone to go out with and to share things with, wouldn't it? And he IS very nice.'

'Never mind that now, I've just seen Gareth.'

'Where? In the bar?'

'Yes—well, leaving rapidly, actually.'

'Did you speak?'

'No, he looked like he was trying to avoid me.'

'How do you feel about it? Are you upset?' said Mags, looking concerned.

'No, not really. I felt a bit odd anyway—probably too much champagne too early in the day!'

Mags looked at her and smiled. 'Yes, that's probably it. You'll feel better when you've had some coffee. Do you want me to wait for you?'

'No, you go back in, I'll be right there.'

Barbara sat on the loo, thinking about the 'exchange that wasn't' between her and Gareth. She hadn't seen him since their divorce had been finalised. She knew it was typical of him to make her feel bad when she was enjoying herself, he'd done it many times when they were together. But what had happened just now was that he'd tried to do this and it had failed. She felt sorry for him, but also recognised that she was now released from the tyranny of his moods. And what about Sean? She was amused that Mags, and for all she knew, Rosalind, had 'picked up' on her flummoxed behaviour at meeting him. Mags was right, of course, she did find him very attractive, and attentive— which was exciting, pleasing and worrying, in equal measure.

Over coffee, Rosalind told Sean that she and Mags had invited a few friends round to their house that evening, and extended the invitation to him. 'And to your girlfriend, partner, or whatever, of course.' To which Sean had replied that he didn't have a girlfriend or partner, and that he would be glad to come.

Barbara had asked some of her musician friends along, at Rosalind's suggestion, and back at the house that afternoon, they set up a couple of gazebos in the garden, and hung some of Barbara's colourful pieces of West African material at the back of one, creating a small 'performance area'. They had put out chairs and small tables, borrowed from the Anthropology Faculty canteen.

Barbara loved these large North Oxford gardens. Rosalind's was typical in that it had a lovely springy lawn, bordered by deep banks of perennials and with several gnarled apple and plum trees as well. Her own garden, at the flat, was equally large and well-established, and she still couldn't believe that she was living in such a place.

With Mags' help, she spent the rest of the afternoon ferrying food she had been preparing for several days from her flat to the house; finishing off dishes and setting it all out. Finally, at about five, she went back to her flat for a nap and to get changed for the party.

When she woke, she had a long hot bath and did some more thinking about Sean, about Gareth, and about Mehmet—the latter she had not heard from for several weeks. She was definitely feeling better about herself and enjoying her life, day-to-day, which had not been the case for a long time. She had always had to have something lined up, something to look forward to, before she felt happy. Now, she realised, she no longer needed to be looking forward all the time, she was content with her life. She thought this odd, at first, considering the situation with Mehmet, but their relationship had changed; he was still very dear to her, and she couldn't deny the passionate nature of their time in Istanbul, but Baku was a different matter entirely. Whenever Barbara now thought of Mehmet, it was always in terms of how she could best help him to get through the mess he'd got himself into. She certainly didn't feel inclined to visit him again in Baku. They had agreed that Mehmet would let her know what was happening out there, whether his plans changed, and of course, when the baby was born. There really didn't seem anything else to say.

And now here she was, getting ready for what she knew would be a lovely evening with good friends, good food and good music—not forgetting the charming Mr Donohue. Barbara's thoughts had seldom ventured further afield than Oxford all day—and central to her thoughts had been largely herself. This was such an unusual state of affairs for someone used to thinking of and worrying about others that it probably contributed at least in part to her overall sense of contentment and well-being.

TWENTY

'It's marvellous, having such a good cook as a friend,' Mags said, returning to the kitchen. 'The tables in the conservatory are laden and it all looks wonderful.'

'Oh I enjoy doing party food, and I don't find it difficult, being a 'foodie',' Barbara laughed in reply.

'If you're all done in here, I think we should go into the garden and have a 'pre-arrival of guests drink' with Rosalind —she's just been trying to cram champagne into the big fridge in the utility room—not much space in there with the punchbowls!'

Mags and Barbara went and rescued Rosalind from the fridge— taking the punchbowls into the conservatory and covering them, leaving far more room for Rosalind's numerous bottles of champagne and Chablis.

'Thank you, girls,' she said, once they were seated around the large patio table. 'You've done a great job, both of you, getting everything ready. The food looks scrumptious and Mags—you've made the conservatory look so pretty with the flowers and everything. I propose a toast—to us!'

She stopped with her glass half raised to her mouth 'Oh look— who's this arriving? It's a little early yet.'

Several men, carrying instrument cases and assorted baggage had appeared at the side of the house and were looking into the garden, unsure of themselves.

'Hey there, yes, you've found us!' Barbara called, going to greet them. 'Hello Joe. OK Bill? Rick, Paul—you're all welcome—come and meet your hosts.'

She took them to meet Rosalind and Mags and then showed them where to set up the small PA system they'd brought along. Mags brought the musicians beer from the kitchen. As she approached Barbara, looking past her, Mag's face lit up 'Sean's here!' she said.

Barbara turned round to find Sean walking towards her carrying a huge bouquet of flowers, as well as a guitar case and a canvas shoulder bag.

'What beautiful flowers!' she said reaching for them as Sean leant to kiss her cheek.

'They're not for you, mind, they're for the ladies who live here, they're my hosts this evening aren't they?'

'Oh! Well, yes, they . . . I suppose so, we . . . I did the food but they live, yes, sorry, I didn't mean to. . . .'

'You should see your face!' he said, laying the flowers down on one of the tables. When he did so it became obvious that there were three separate bunches. 'It's OK—there are enough for all of you—no squabbling now! I'm sorry, I shouldn't tease.'

Barbara felt awkward—she had been embarrassed and then felt that he was making fun of her. She didn't know what to say and wanted simply to get away. She turned from him and started to walk quickly across the lawn to the house, calling back to Sean 'I'll go and tell Rosalind you're here.'

She went into the kitchen and drank a glass of water. She looked out through the window onto the lawns and could see that Rosalind was already out there, talking and laughing with Mags and Sean. She knew that her friends would not laugh at her maliciously and told herself that she was over-reacting. It had just been a joke, a little at her expense but no big deal. She went out again to the garden, by which time guests seemed to be arriving all at once and she found herself busily propelled from one group to another for well over an hour. The music was going well, her friends performing a mixture of English, Irish and Scottish tunes and songs. At a break between tunes, Rosalind had gone to a microphone and urged people to help themselves to food in the conservatory, so a little while later, Barbara went there to see if any of the platters needed replenishing. As she crossed to the kitchen, she heard the musicians start an Irish tune she loved—*Si Bheag Si Mhor*, not a tune she had heard Joe, Bill and the others do before, although she often urged them to. She went to the window and saw that all of the guests had stopped chatting and were looking at the 'stage', where Sean was playing guitar, accompanied by Rick on fiddle. It was beautiful. She closed her eyes and let the music flow through her. Always, the heartbreakingly-wonderful swoop of the music as it built and built to its finish made her eyes prick with tears—the tune had always made her think of her father, and since her mother died, Barbara thought of the both of them every time she heard it.

It was over; people were clapping and the other musicians whistling and shouting 'More!' and 'Good job!' Barbara went to the kitchen and started taking more canapés and sandwiches from the fridge. She turned to the table and was startled to see Sean standing in the doorway.

'Oh—Sean, that was really beautiful just now. I love that tune so much. Thanks for playing it.'

'Look—did I upset you earlier?' he said, ignoring the compliment. 'About the flowers I mean. You disappeared and I didn't see you after that. It was just me having a bit of fun y'know. I'm sorry if you thought I was making fun of you.'

'It's OK, I was just embarrassed really, and it would have been awful if they had been just for the others and I'd assumed . . . but no, I'm OK, it's stupid of me to feel upset. I'm sorry I was childish and ran away.'

'I knew I shouldn't have teased you—when you went in I was going to come to find you, then I felt bad because I'd made a bit of a prick of myself and thought I'd better just join in with the lads and stay out there. I was just asking Rick if there was a tune he knew you liked, and *all* of them said: '*Si Bheag Si Mhor*'! They said you were always fed up with them because they don't play it in their usual repertoire, but Rick knows it, so offered to give it a go with me. I hoped you'd hear it—it's my peace offering. Shall you accept it and we can be friends again?'

'Oh Sean, is that really true? That's so sweet of you. Of course I accept it.'

'I think the flowers were all 'merged' by Mags though—she took them and I saw her later walk by with a great enormous vase full of them!'

'It doesn't matter, they'll be here for everyone to enjoy—I can take some home tonight I'm sure.'

'What are you doing now anyway? *Always find me in the kitchen at parties*', is it?'

'I was just putting out more food, but I'm done now. These need to go to the conservatory, then I'd like to sit and listen to some more music outside.'

Sean took one of the platters and followed Barbara to the conservatory. 'Will you be singing tonight?' he asked her.

'Oh god, no,' she replied. 'I do only unaccompanied songs, usually, and while we've got the guys here with their gear I'm sure people would rather listen to 'proper' music. We can't expect all Rosalind and Mags' friends to appreciate what we 'folkies' like!'

'You sing 'Who Knows Where the Time Goes' don't you?'

'Yes, but like I said . . .'

'Well I can play it, why don't you sing it with me? Or even better, why not have Rick play as well, and he can do some twiddly-fiddley stuff in the middle that they'll probably like?'

'I don't know, I hadn't thought of it. None of these people has heard me sing. I'm not sure.'

'Then how about we go and have a few drinks and listen a while,' he said, placing his hand on her shoulder and steering her towards the garden. 'And then we can collar Rick and come inside for a quick rehearsal. If it's no good, we shan't do it.'

As soon as they went outside they realised that a 'come-all-ye'/open-mike session had already started up, replacing the more organised and rehearsed music. One of Rosalind's colleagues—one of 'the Profs'—was speaking to the musicians and then launched into a lively song in Italian, with bawdy lyrics that Rosalind took delight in translating for those whose Italian was not up to it. It was a great hit with everyone.

'See? It'll be just like a session from now on—I knew the lads hadn't that long a set planned!' Sean said.

'Come on, why don't we do a song or two?'

Mags overheard this and clapped her hands together like an excited schoolgirl. 'Ooh yes! Are you going to sing, Barbara? I'd love to hear you.' And turning, she called across the lawn: 'Rosalind, Barbara's going to sing!'

'Talk about being put on the spot,' Barbara said. 'I'd like to wait a while, Mags, and we have to rehearse a bit first, so don't get everyone expecting us just yet.'

'You're going to sing with Sean? Both of you? Ooh that's even better!' she said and went tripping off to join Rosalind and a group of their friends.

Sean was right, after the 'Prof' had sung, the musicians were approached by several of the guests who were willing to perform their 'party pieces', and others who requested particular songs or tunes. A hugely diverse mixture was performed that evening; from classical pieces to Gilbert and Sullivan, to Beatles numbers, Simon and Garfunkel, and always back to the 'folkie' standards that Barbara knew so well. She and Sean had joined in with the others, singing several Irish songs from the stage area, to Mag's delight, before going with Rick to the drawing room to run through the song suggested by Sean earlier.

Several years running, at Fairport Convention's Cropredy Festivals, Barbara had experienced the huge waves of emotion that engulfed the crowds when *'Who Knows Where the Time Goes'* was played during the final set. It was guaranteed to have most of the festival audience shedding tears and hugging complete strangers next to them in the crowd in 'folkie camaraderie'. But that happened to Barbara only at Cropredy—she could sing or hear the song perfectly calmly at other venues. So she hadn't reckoned on the effect that the Sandy Denny classic would have on Rosalind.

She had to admit that the song went well, and was surprised that after drinking quite a lot of champagne and red wine that her voice felt so clear—perhaps it helped—but afterwards, when the guests were applauding, she noticed that Mags had her arms around Rosalind, who seemed to be upset. Barbara went over to them.

'Are you all right?' she asked.

'Oh dear, yes,' Rosalind replied, dabbing her face with a napkin. 'So silly of me, dear, but you sang that so beautifully and the words just make one think about everything that has happened—and that is yet to happen, too, don't they? I just found myself in floods of tears! But well done, and thank you. The music has been so enjoyable and it was thanks to you that all these marvellously talented people came along. Come on, Mags, let's go and 'mingle' a bit—people are looking over at me—I want to assure them that I'm just being silly and sentimental and it's nothing to worry about!'

'Ach, the power of a great song!' Sean was by Barbara's side and handed her a glass of wine.

'Thank you. I didn't know you were there, did you hear what she said?'

'Most of it. She's OK though, I'm sure. Good song—went well didn't it? You should sing accompanied songs more often.'

'I enjoyed it and they seemed to as well,' she said, nodding at the guests. 'I think we can leave it to the others now though, I could do with sitting down for a while.' They went over to the largest tree at the edge of the lawn, which had a seat built around its trunk.

'That's better,' she said, slipping off her sandals and sitting with her feet up on the seat, her arms around her knees. 'I love this garden. And Oxford—I've always loved Oxford because of all this . . . the people you get here, I mean. I call it my 'home town' although I guess it's not, really, I was twelve years old before I moved here.'

'Tell me about how you came to be here, then,' said Sean, 'Look, I'll sit here, and if you turn a bit, that's it, you can lean back on me—I'm a wee bit softer than the old bark.'

And so they stayed, swapping their histories, until the small hours, when the last remaining guests began to gather their things and take their leave.

TWENTY ONE

They learned much about one another that evening. It was a beautiful night, fairly warm for the start of May, enabling the guests to remain until late in the garden, sitting in candlelit groups here and there around tables, chatting quietly and happily. Sean had 'done the rounds', making sure their drinks were topped up, each time he went to get drinks, and later, coffee, for himself and Barbara.

She watched him talking and laughing with the guests, and smiled at his easy charm with everyone. *'Including me,'* she thought. She had found it so easy to talk with Sean that she had told him pretty much all there was to tell about her life so far, including her marriage to Gareth, her divorce, and her relationship with Mehmet. Sean had listened without interrupting her while she spoke, asking only a few questions when she came to breaks in her story. He didn't seem the least bit shocked or judgemental about her 'adventures' during her travels. He did ask whether she hoped to 'further her relationship' with Mehmet, despite his current situation. Barbara was able to tell him, honestly, that she doubted if she and Mehmet would be lovers again, although she didn't know why she felt so sure about that.

In turn, Barbara learned that Sean came from Donegal. Unusually for the region of his birth, he was an only son, and like her, both his parents were now dead. He had studied Anthropology at Oxford, and then returned to Ireland for a while, and became involved with the running of courses at the Gaeltacht Cultural Centre. He was about to return there 'more or less' permanently, he told her, to take up a job which would allow him to live 'properly' in the cottage he had inherited from his parents.

'It's no mansion,' he'd said when describing it. 'But I love it there, the views are grand. The hills go right down to the sea. There's land around the house—about three acres. I let my neighbour graze his sheep in one of the fields, and his wife looks after the chickens and keeps an eye on the place when I'm not there.'

'Don't' laugh,' Barbara said, 'but I've always wanted to keep chickens.'

'I'll not laugh at you for that. I love having them about, and the other animals; the sheep and the like. I might get a dog now that I'm going to be there more often. Do you like dogs?'

'More of a cat person, really, but I like all animals—sometimes far more than humans!'

'Aye, I'm with you there,' Sean laughed. 'That's why the house is good—it can be full of folks if you want to ask them in, but it's in its own place; if you want to shut the door and be quiet, that's fine, too.'

'It sounds like a place at peace with itself.' Barbara said when he'd told her about his home.

'That's a fine way of describing it, I like that. You'll have to come over and see it for yourself—in between all your travelling, if you'd like to?'

She told him that she'd love to visit him in Ireland, in fact, she had been longing to go there since her father died, long ago. She wanted to trace her father's family, but was a little afraid that she was fond of 'the idea' of Ireland without having been there to experience the reality of it. Sean had appreciated her honesty about this—they talked about the work he was doing at the Cultural Centre, though which he saw plenty of what he called the 'Born Again Irish'—those 'heritage tourists', mainly from America, desperate for a sense of kinship and of belonging.

He said that Barbara was welcome to stay with him in Donegal whenever she needed to research her family history, as Belfast, her father's birthplace, was not that far from his home.

By one in the morning, the last of the guests had left, and Barbara and Sean went around the garden with Rosalind and Mags, clearing up glasses and the usual after-party debris. Barbara packed away the remains of the buffet, tidied up the kitchen, loaded the dishwasher, and then made tea for the four of them, which they drank sitting around the kitchen table, chatting about the party.

Sean lived in the Jericho area of Oxford, not that much further on from Barbara's flat, and at his suggestion, they shared a taxi home. He wouldn't hear of her contributing to the fare, however, and after a very chaste, but tender kiss on both cheeks, he left, saying he would call her the next day to see if she felt like 'doing something' for the rest of the day after she had been back to Rosalind's to finish clearing up.

Barbara noticed her answerphone light flashing when she walked into her hallway, but decided to make a cup of tea and 'get in' before listening to it. When she did, she at first thought it was Mehmet, but realised that it was Şerif, Gul's brother, saying that Mehmet had given him the number—hoped she didn't mind 'the contacting', but that he was definitely going to be in London in the summer, visiting his friend in Stoke-New-ing-ton (he enunciated this very deliberately, which made Barbara smile), and that he would very much like to meet up with her if she would like to. He left no number, and Barbara thought it a little odd that he would phone with this message so far in advance of his intended visit.

The last thing she remembered thinking before sleep overtook her was how she had not thought about Mehmet all evening. Sure, she had spoken to Sean about him, but he wasn't 'taking up headspace' in the way he once did; she didn't find herself wondering what he was doing, several times each day. But then the message from Şerif had been like a little 'call', a small reminder of what had gone before.

The following day, the Tuesday, she went back to Rosalind and Mag's house to clear up and have the inevitable post-mortem about the party. Rosalind was as cheekily complimentary about Sean as she had been in Istanbul about Mehmet. And Mags was chirping away like an excited fledgling about him. In an attempt to stop their questions and chattering, Barbara told them that she and Sean were going to meet up before he left for Ireland, and surprisingly, this seemed to do the trick. Back at home, she was pottering about the garden when she heard the phone ring. It was Sean, who suggested they went out to eat that night.

He arrived at 7.30 and had already ordered a taxi for 7.45 to take them to The Trout at Wolvercote Bridge. Barbara had always liked the pub, with its peacocks strutting on the riverside patio, but had not eaten in the restaurant before. The food was lovely, and unusually for the time of year, the pub was not crowded.

They talked of everything and nothing. Barbara couldn't later remember much of their conversation, except that Sean told her that he was leaving from Heathrow on the following Friday, and she had immediately offered to take him to the airport in her car. She was aware of a small voice in her head saying '*Here we go again, more airports; more departures.*'

But she pushed the thought away. They sat on the patio after their meal, with coffee and cognac. Barbara felt so content, with the noise of the river rushing through the bridge, the occasional sudden, loud, 'quack' from the ducks, sounding as if one had been rudely surprised; and now and then the wonderful call of the peacocks. She didn't feel the excitement or anticipation that she had felt in similar situations with Mehmet; it didn't feel awkward at all, just natural and 'comfortable'.

It wasn't until later, back at her flat, that she felt the awkwardness so often associated with 'coming back for coffee' on first dates.

They had walked around the garden, Barbara pointing out what she had done to it since moving in, and telling Sean what she wanted to do with it next. They drank coffee in the lounge, listening to a tape of Irish folk bands that Sean had brought and given to her.

'It's been a lovely couple of days, Sean, thanks so much,' she said.

'Well, thanks to you, too, it's been grand. But it's getting late so I'd better be on my way,' Sean replied, standing up. 'Think I'll walk home, unless I could . . .'

'Yes, of course you can stay!' Barbara blurted out, as she, too, stood up next to him.

'I . . . erm . . . well, actually I was going to ask if I could use your phone to call a taxi!'

Barbara sat down on the sofa again. 'Oh fuck!' she groaned, her hands over her face. 'Oh no, this is awful. I can't believe I said that. It's not even that I . . .'

Sean crouched down in front of her, his hands on her shoulders. 'Sure it's all right,' he said, soothingly. 'Really, come on, don't be daft, you just said what I'd been thinking but I wasn't the one to suggest it, that's all.'

'No, it's not all right,' she said, taken her hands from her face and looking at him. 'You see, I'm not sure it's what I want. Oh that sounded wrong. What I mean is that you're about to leave and will be in Donegal, and I've had enough of long-distance relationships, and despite all that I go and shoot my mouth off like that so you'll be thinking I want to drag you off to bed.'

'Well I'd take it as a compliment if you did want to,' Sean said. 'To be honest with you, the only reason I haven't 'come on' to you in that way is exactly as you say, I'm off in a few days, and you're here. And even if we slept together for the next few nights, it would seem like a kind of 'one-night stand' type of thing, and I don't want it to be like that between us.'

'Thanks,' Barbara said. 'And you may take the compliment.'

He looked at her quizzically, his head on one side.

'You said you'd take it as a compliment if I wanted to go to bed with you. Well, I would. I do. But . . . oh now I feel awkward and embarrassed.'

Sean stood up, taking her hands and pulling her to her feet as well.

'Come here,' he said, and drew her to him. Barbara's head was against his chest; he leant the side of his face against her hair. 'Listen, I'm really glad I've met you, and I'd like to hope that we can see more of each other in the future, but I don't want either of us to be sad that we're about to part. I've been putting things in place for this move and the job for quite a while, and it's what I want to do. And you've just been through a lot of changes in your life too. You've been telling me how much you like the flat and how happy you've been feeling—so neither of us should be sad about anything. We'll stay in touch—come over and see me in Donegal, it's really not far away is it? Neither of us is planning to emigrate to the other side of the planet now, are we? And what will be, will be. None of us knows what's in store for us.'

Barbara looked up at him. 'Thanks,' she said. 'And yes, you're right. It's just a bit of a bugger meeting you right now. But we mustn't wish things were other than they are when we don't know how things will pan out in the future. We're both of us feeling fortunate with our lot at the moment aren't we?' Sean leant down and kissed her tenderly on the lips.

'And now that I've done that I really must go,' he said, smiling. 'Or we'll end up in bed and make a mockery of all our fine words.'

TWENTY TWO

July 1995

'Slainte from Donegal!

Hope everything's fine with you. The house was a bit cold and damp when I arrived, but is all right now. Some good things planned at the Centre—concerts and the like, will write you about it all soon, maybe you'd like to come over for some of them?

Give my love to Rosalind & Mags,

And take some for yourself, of course,

Stay lovely as you are,

Sean'

Barbara received Sean's first postcard the Wednesday after he'd left. She took him to Heathrow, where they'd had lunch in a noisy café before saying goodbye at the Departures gate. It hadn't been a wrenching, tearful goodbye such as she'd experienced with Mehmet at all. With Sean she felt happy, and optimistic about their lives—separate though they might be. Since then, she and Sean had exchanged many letters and phone calls, and had begun to talk about Barbara visiting him for a holiday.

While Sean was obviously thriving in his new role at the Cultural Centre, Barbara was beginning to feel unsettled in her own job. She had been working with the 'Emergencies' team responsible for humanitarian work in the war-torn former Yugoslavia, which gave her daily access to the most distressing information and stories that never made it into the newspapers in the UK. And things were changing within the organisation she worked for: US-inspired 'ways of working' (with the attendant 'management-speak'); departmental restructurings; and the speedy comings and goings of 'career charity workers' were making it a very different place in which to work. Several long-standing friends and colleagues had already left and gone to work elsewhere. This was particularly difficult for her coming as it did when everything else in her 'home' life was so much better than it had been for years. But although unsettling, Barbara could not imagine working anywhere else, especially if it were to involve moving away, permanently, from Oxford.

She had received only one letter from Mehmet since May. In it, he had told her that Gul had been in hospital in Istanbul for a few days but that she (and the baby) were all right and she was back at home with her mother. He told her about his job at the casino and bits and pieces about his everyday life, but there was no hint of the intimacy they had once shared, nothing of the sweet, romantic letters she used to receive from him. Barbara talked with Rosalind about Mehmet's letter and, ever the stoic, Rosalind had advised that she just 'go with the flow', do nothing and let things 'roll on' for a while. 'These things have a way of working themselves out, dear,' she'd said. 'And none of us knows what is around the next corner.'

Barbara smiled. 'Now you're sounding like Sean,' she said.

'Then he is obviously a very wise young man, just as I have always believed him to be,' replied Rosalind, patting Barbara's hand.

Early the following Friday evening, Barbara came in from the garden to answer her phone.

'Hallo? Barbara? It is Şerif. I am here in London.'

'*Merhaba* Şerif! I'm glad you got here at last. How are you?'

'I am fine, thank you. Can you come to London?'

'Well, yes, I'm sure I'll be able to meet you while you're here, how long are staying?'

'Will you come tomorrow?'

Barbara was a little taken aback by this, but couldn't think of any reason why not, she had no other plans, so she said she would go up by bus the next morning and they arranged to meet at Manor House tube station at mid-day.

Every time Barbara went to London by bus she spent the last part of the journey looking out at the houses and blocks of flats lining the dual carriageway and thinking how much she would hate to live in one of them. She just *had* to have a garden, no matter how small, and preferably away from traffic—certainly away from the twenty-four hour, exhaust-fugged rumble that was always outside the front door of these homes. She loathed London, and went there as seldom as possible. It wasn't so bad, she thought, if there was a specific venue one was heading for, going to a specific event, but on days like this, when she was having to navigate across the city to an area she had never before visited, she quickly became fed up with the crowds, and with being jostled, pushed, and having her feet trodden on. She felt far too hot, and several times wished she'd not agreed to meet Şerif in London at all. So she wasn't feeling at her best when she eventually arrived at Manor House tube station and stepped out onto the street.

She spotted Şerif at once. He was leaning with his back against the wall just outside the station entrance, smoking a cigarette. He saw her, tossed the cigarette away and came towards her. '*Merhaba*, I am pleased to see you, Barbara,' he said, presenting her with a small bunch of freesias.

'*Merhaba* Şerif, hello. Oh that's sweet of you, thank you.'

There followed an awkward moment when Şerif went to shake hands—Barbara took his hand and moved to kiss his cheek, but he stepped back, causing her to stumble towards him.

'I'm gasping for a drink,' she said quickly, to hide her embarrassment. Shall we go over there?' She pointed at a café across the road with tables outside.

'Yes, we can go there,' Şerif replied, and guiding her by her elbow, they crossed the road and sat down at one of the tables. Şerif ordered a Coke while Barbara had a lager. They chatted about Şerif's journey; he told her about his friends in London and how he knew the various families. Barbara was aware that neither of them had mentioned Mehmet.

'I will take you to my friend Yaman's place for lunch,' Şerif said.

'It is a very nice place, very popular. You will like it. You will think you are in Istanbul again!'

'I felt like that when I was in Baku,' Barbara replied. But she looked away from Şerif, feeling awkward even mentioning the place, as if all that had happened between her and Mehmet on her last visit there was suddenly laid bare. It immediately became 'the elephant in the room' and Barbara decided to tackle it straight away.

'How is your sister? Mehmet wrote to me that she had been in hospital in Istanbul.'

'She is fine, it was just for the doctors to check her over, but she is OK. She waits for the baby now at my mother's house. It will come next month.'

'Yes, I *know* when the baby is due, Şerif,' she said rather sharply. She felt annoyed with him but wasn't sure why. Perhaps because he spoke of Gul and the baby without any acknowledgement of Barbara's 'involvement'—as if her relationship with Mehmet had not existed. He could have been telling just anyone about his sister, and Barbara did not feel that she was 'just anyone' in this particular series of events.

'I am sorry, you do not want to talk about it? But you asked me,' said Şerif, looking confused by Barbara's tone.

'No, forgive me, Şerif, it's me who should be sorry. I just find it a bit odd, you and I meeting up—whether we talk about Mehmet, Gul, and what has happened or whether we avoid the subject, either way, it's odd.'

'Are you very angry with them? I think you are hating Gul, because of the baby. She is very stupid to be in this situation.'

'I don't hate her. I can't think of anyone I've ever hated, unless it's Margaret Thatcher and what she did to this country! But seriously, I'm not even angry with Mehmet anymore—I was at first. I feel sorry that he was stupid enough to get in this situation, one that will prob- ably affect the rest of his life, but I don't hate either of them. I'm concerned . . . worried about them more than anything else.'

'I know Mehmet is sad he hurt you, that you are not together,' said Şerif.

'We never were 'together', really, though, were we? Just when we were in Istanbul. Maybe we would have been, one day. I know he thought about that sometimes.' Barbara pushed the contents of the ashtray around with her cigarette.

'He used to say in his letters that he wondered if we might be together in the future. But now he doesn't write very often, and when we do exchange letters, or occasionally speak on the phone, it's not like it was. I think of him as a friend now, not really as a 'boyfriend' or lover.'

'He does not love my sister. We all know this. Maybe you will find another boyfriend? But come, we must go and have our lunch.' Şerif stood up, went into the café and paid their bill, and then they set off for the restaurant which was, he told her, one of many Turkish places on Stoke Newington High Street.

Şerif was right about Barbara feeling like she was in Istanbul. As they neared their destination, every other shop, restaurant or café was Turkish. She heard the language spoken by people in the street, and there were large posters in most shop windows advertising chcap flights to Turkish cities. Yaman's restaurant, *Lalezar*, meaning 'Tulip Garden', was rather smart-looking, on two floors; Turkish 'Arabesque' music played loudly, and everyone seemed in high-spirits. Şerif greeted several people as they entered, and then introduced her to Yaman himself, who came from behind the bar to greet them. He was very tall, about thirty years old, Barbara estimated, and extremely good-looking.

'Ah! Here is the Oxford Turkish lady!' he said, coming towards Barbara. 'Hoş geldiniz!'

'Hoş bulduk!' she replied, quickly remembering the standard response. Yaman shook her hand and kissed her on both cheeks— without the awkwardness there had been earlier when she and Şerif greeted one another.

'Come, I give you special table, here,' Yaman continued, indicating an oval table at the back of the room, in front of glass doors which gave, improbably, onto a pretty courtyard garden.

Barbara and Şerif sat down. Several waiters proceeded to bring them dish after dish of delicious Turkish *mezes*, along with two large jugs—one of *raki*, one of water—as the traditional accompaniment.

'This is fabulous,' Barbara said, half-way through their meal. 'But I'd forgotten how strong the *raki* is, it's gone to my head already.' Şerif looked puzzled, so she explained: 'You know, I mean, it makes you feel drunk very quickly.'

'It does not make me drunk so fast,' he replied. 'Maybe it is because I drink it from when very young. At weddings and parties with my family. It is tradition in Turkey.'

'I can never work out who drinks alcohol and who doesn't—of my Turkish friends, I mean. Most of the people I've met seem to. But if you'll excuse me, I'm just nipping to the 'Ladies'—do you know where it is? *Tuvelet nerede?*'

Şerif told her, and she made her way rather unsteadily to the loo, where she felt hot and dizzy, and was violently sick.

TWENTY THREE

Barbara woke and pulled the duvet more closely around her. She looked around the room from where she lay. Several clothes-horses draped with drying nappies and babies' clothing; a huge TV set on the floor; several cardboard boxes.

'*Oh for fuck's sake,*' she thought to herself. '*This is bloody awful, and it's all my own fault.*' She sat up, carefully, checking how she felt, and was relieved to find that she no longer had a raging headache. She looked at her watch and was shocked to see it was eight o'clock. She began to get up and gather her things together, her bag was on the floor with one of her sandals. She had no idea where the other one was.

Having thrown up in the loo at lunchtime, she had spent quite a while in there, rinsing her mouth, splashing cold water on her face and holding her wrists under the running tap in the attempt to cool down and sober up, but she still felt dreadful; the most awful headache pounded at every move she made. Several times, someone came and tried the door, other female customers, she guessed. She didn't know what was worse—staying in the loo and causing people to wonder why she was in there so long, or to leave its sanctuary and have to face everyone, including Şerif and Yaman, in the state she was in. Eventually, she heard someone knocking on the outer door.

'Barbara, are you all right? Can I help you?' Şerif's voice called quietly.

She'd felt no option but to open the door and to admit to him that she had been and was still feeling very unwell. Şerif helped her to walk through the restaurant, (which she later cringed to think back on, as all the other diners were looking at them, and especially her, she felt, disapprovingly). He guided her up two flights of stairs to the flat Yaman shared with his wife, Zeliha, and their three-month-old baby son. Barbara told Şerif that she wanted just to lie down for a little while, she was sure that she would be OK after that. So having only just met, Zeliha led Barbara, shyly, to a room with a single bed in it, drew the curtains across, and left Barbara to sleep, 'You need anything, you call, OK?' she said as she left the room.

That must have been at about three o'clock at the latest, she thought. And now it was eight—she had intended to be back in Oxford by now, instead of which she was in a strange bedroom, in the home of people she didn't know. The more she thought about what had happened, the more embarrassed she felt. At such times, all that matters is to get home—to have the comfort of your own, familiar things around you. If only it were possible to 'transport' oneself instantly, instead of actually having to get it together to travel home. Waiting at bus stops, checking timetables, and enduring the journey itself seems impossible when all one wants to do is curl up, pretend nothing is wrong, and sleep.

She listened for a moment, and could hear voices close by, as well as a general 'hubbub' coming from the restaurant downstairs. She went to the door and opened it slightly; a conversation was going on, in rapid Turkish, in the room opposite. Barbara stepped back into the bedroom and was just about to shut the door quietly when she trod on her stray sandal, stumbled, and putting her hand out to save herself, leant against the door heavily, causing it to bang shut. The conversation stopped abruptly.

'Barbara? Are you all right? Are you awake?' Şerif's voice called to her.

She opened the door to him. 'Yes, sorry, I tripped over my sandal,' she said. 'I can't believe how late it is, I should have been home by now. I'm so sorry about all this.'

'It is OK,' said Şerif. 'But are you feeling all right now? Come into the room here, with Zeliha and me. We have news, come.'

Barbara padded into the sitting room in her bare feet. Zeliha was laying her baby down in a small folding pram. 'Arif is sleeping now,' she said. 'How are you, Barbara? I hope you are OK? I will make some tea—would you like tea?'

'That would be lovely, thank you. I am so sorry to put you out like this. I am ashamed of myself.'

'It does not matter,' Zeliha replied. 'Do not worry.' And she went to the kitchen, pausing as she passed Şerif in the doorway to say something to him quietly in Turkish.

Barbara sat down on the sofa and looked up at Şerif. 'I really have ruined the day and made a fool of myself,' she said.

Şerif smiled and sat on the coffee table opposite her. He covered her hands with his.

'It was not really your fault,' he said. 'I should not have let you have too much *raki*. It is not good to have it at lunchtime.'

'I should have been the one to stop myself drinking it!' Barbara replied. 'And I'd had that beer at the café, earlier. Whatever must Yaman and Zeliha think of me?'

Şerif laughed. 'Well, I told him that it was not his food that made you ill,' he said.

'Oh god! Of course it wasn't! How awful, eating in his lovely restaurant and then being ill! Poor man, I hope he didn't really think that, not even for a moment. It doesn't look good, for a restaurant owner, does it? Someone being ill after eating your food. I'd much rather the other diners just wrote me off as an old "lush" than thought it was anything to do with the food!'

'What is "lush"?' Şerif asked.

'It is a drunkard—someone who drinks too much.'

Zeliha returned with the tea—in mugs for her and Barbara, and a small glass of it, without milk, for Şerif. She looked meaningfully at Şerif as she set the tray on the table.

Şerif cleared his throat. 'We had a phone call while you were sleeping,' he said. 'From my mother in Istanbul. My sister went to the hospital and she had her baby this afternoon, at four o'clock. It is a boy.'

'What? What do you mean? It can't be . . . it's not due 'til next month. Is it all right? Is she . . . is Gul all right? Oh—I don't know what to say!' Barbara gabbled with the shock of the news.

'Yes, it is born early, but they are both fine. It is very small baby but he is well.' Şerif said, his eyes fixed on Barbara's. 'It is a very good hospital, where they are, very modern, and they will be fine.' He passed a mug of tea to her. 'What about you?'

'Me? I'm OK now I've had a sleep, it was just the *raki*, like you said.'

'No, that is not what I mean. I mean about the baby,' he said.

'It's unexpected news, I must say,' Barbara sipped her tea. 'I'm pleased that they are both all right. But look, what are you going to do? Are you going back to Istanbul early now? You must have lots to think about, and I shouldn't be here, either, taking up your time.'

'No, I will return on the flight I booked already,' he said. 'I am not needed at home. My mother said it is all right for me to stay as I planned. I will go home next month.'

'But I should get back to Oxford,' Barbara said. 'I have no idea what time I'll get home now. I know the times of the buses from Marble Arch, but I'll have to get there as soon as possible. Can I call a taxi?'

Zeliha was at the pram, gently tucking a sheet over her baby. She touched her son's cheek tenderly as he stirred in his sleep. She straightened up and turned to Barbara. 'You are welcome to stay here tonight,' she said. 'You have not been well, and it is not good to travel now. Please stay.'

'Oh Zeliha, that's very sweet of you, but I don't want to trouble you any more than I have already,' Barbara said, standing up and putting her empty mug on the table.

Şerif stood up at the same time and placed his hand on her shoulder.

'Zeliha is right,' he said. 'It will be no trouble, there is plenty of room, and we would all like you to stay. Yaman said he was sorry he could not spend time with you today. If you stay, we will all have pleasant time together tonight, when the restaurant is finished, and tomorrow, I will take you to get your bus home.'

'But I haven't got anything with me,' Barbara turned towards Zeliha. 'I didn't bring an overnight bag!'

Zeliha smiled. 'There is a shop near here—you can buy toothbrush, maybe?' she said. 'And I will lend you night clothes, if you need?'

Barbara looked from Zeliha to Şerif; at their smiling faces, encouraging her to agree to their suggestion.

'Well, thank you, I will stay, if you are quite sure it's not a bother. I had better go and investigate the shop for a toothbrush then, and on the way, I will go and show Yaman that I am still alive, and apologise for my earlier behaviour!'

TWENTY FOUR

That evening was one of the most uncomfortable that Barbara could remember. It was a warm night, and about ten pm, an hour or so before the restaurant closed, she helped Zeliha to lay up a large table out in the courtyard garden, where they were all to eat when Zaman and his staff had finished work. A little water fountain babbled in the corner. *'So many meals I've had outside, in pretty courtyards,'* she thought to herself as she placed cutlery on the table. *'With so many different people.'* She sighed, thinking of Mehmet and how distant he had sounded on the phone earlier. She felt a strange kind of embarrassment for just being there, on that day, with all these Turkish people who knew Mehmet and probably his situation—maybe even that they had been lovers?

It had been Şerif's idea to call Mehmet, he admitted afterwards, 'to tell him about the baby'. But his mother had already phoned Şerif's brother, Nurettin, in Baku, and so Mehmet had known before even Şerif had received the news. In the sitting room, Şerif had been speaking loudly and excitedly into the phone, and before Barbara knew what was happening, he passed the phone to her—it was only then that she realised that it was Mehmet.

'Barbara? Hello. It is strange that you are there. How are you?'

'Mehmet, love, hello. And congratulations, you have a son it seems. Şerif says that they are both fine, so that's good. I should be back in Oxford, but I got ill on *raki*—it was embarrassing—but everyone . . .'

'Şerif told me.' Mehmet cut her short, something he had never done before. 'Are you staying there with Şerif tonight?'

'What? Yes, well, no, I'm staying with Yaman and his wife, what do you mean?'

'Sorry, no, I did not mean anything, I was worried you would be upset and not at home with your friends.'

'Mehmet, I'm not upset about the baby, OK? I've got used to the idea over the last few months. I'm more upset after being ill at lunchtime, actually. What are your plans now? You can't go to Istanbul, can you?'

'No, but when the baby is a little bigger, Gul will bring him here, to Baku, to stay with Nurettin's family—until I can find somewhere for us to live.'

He sounded so matter-of-fact about it. Barbara realised that he had probably resigned himself to the whole 'marriage and family' thing and it wasn't the time or the place to have a deeper conversation with him about it all.

'Well,' she said quickly, 'I mustn't keep you on the phone, it must be costing Yaman a lot of money, so I'll put Şerif back on the line, OK? Take care of yourself.'

'I will write to you,' he said, but Barbara didn't say anything else, she passed the phone back to Şerif, who resumed the loud Turkish "banter" with his friend. When he hung up, he turned to Barbara, his face flushed.

'Well, it is all happy for them!' he said.

Barbara glared at him. 'Şerif, I didn't find that very easy, y'know. I wish you had told me that you were talking to Mehmet, and you could have asked me before shoving the phone at me like that.'

'But you said that you are OK about the baby and everything—earlier, you said you were not upset? I am sorry, I thought it was OK.'

Barbara raised her hand in a gesture that said 'enough'.

'It's just not that simple,' she said, rising. 'I'm going to help Zeliha, I'll see you later.'

'*If only it were that simple*', she thought, as she spread the tablecloth on the table. Traits in others, which at first seem endearing, can sometimes infuriate, and Barbara was finding this increasingly true of her Turkish friends, the more she spent time with them. It was the way they take everything so literally—'you said it was OK so it's OK' kind of stuff—no subtle nuance of feeling or emotion.

Barbara sighed. She was tired of having to remember Turkish words, phrases, etiquette; tired of having to think about how to express herself in English in ways that could be easily understood; tired of misunderstandings. She'd felt this before, when she'd been on work trips of three weeks or more, but was surprised to find herself feeling like it after just one day in London with Şerif and his friends. She felt a bit guilty, feeling like this when surrounded by such hospitable people, but couldn't help it. It made her realise that one of the nicest things about spending time with Sean was that she could forget all of that and as a consequence, she felt far more relaxed in his company. She smiled to herself as she remembered that there had, actually, been a couple of 'misunderstandings' with Sean—the flowers at the garden party, which was just him teasing; and the time she'd blurted out that he could stay the night when he was going to call a taxi—a bit embarrassing, that one, but they laughed about it a lot, before he left for Ireland. None of that had been caused by a language or culture 'barrier' though. She would like to spend more time in his easy company again, one day. But for now, she had to do her best to get through the rest of the evening before she could escape back to Oxford and the sanctuary of her flat as early as possible the next day.

She was relieved to find that she was actually quite hungry and looking forward to the meal by the time they all sat down. There was a lot of good-natured leg-pulling about Yaman having poisoned Şerif's guest, which everyone took in good part. But Şerif seemed determined to 'celebrate' the birth of his nephew, and during the meal mentioned the baby far more than Barbara would have liked. Yaman seemed to sense this, and that it was making Barbara uncomfortable, for several times he noticeably changed the subject of the conversation; he and Barbara exchanged glances a few times, when, she hoped, she conveyed her gratitude for his thoughtfulness.

'He is to be called "Ateş",' Şerif announced at one point, standing up with a glass of *raki* in his hand. 'It is a fine name, a strong name, in English it is meaning "Fire",' he said, turning to Barbara. 'We will all drink toast now, to my nephew, Ateş.'

Barbara put her hand over her empty glass. 'Forgive me, but I don't think I will be touching *raki* again for quite some time,' she said quietly to Yaman and Zeliha, who were sitting either side of her. 'But I will raise my glass of water instead.'

Zeliha patted Barbara's hand and smiled. Then she said something to Yaman in Turkish before turning back to Barbara. 'Will you help to make tea, Barbara? Or coffee if you would like? I must check on Arif, so if you would start to make things ready in the kitchen down-stairs—in the restaurant, I will come when I have seen the baby.'

Barbara was glad to leave the table. She followed Zeliha into the restaurant kitchen and was shown where to find what she needed to make the drinks. She filled a very large kettle, put it onto the range and lit the gas under it, before setting out *chai* glasses on their tiny glass saucers, along with some mugs for anyone who preferred them. Zeliha returned.

'He is fine, sleeping,' she said. 'I hope you are all right, Barbara? Şerif is not sensitive to you, I think? Yaman is going to speak to him.'

'Oh there's no need for him to do that,' Barbara said quickly. Then realising what Zeliha had said, she added 'Zeliha, do I take it that you all know about my relationship with Mehmet?'

'Not everyone, just Yaman and me. The staff know only that you are a friend of Şerif. It is all right, Barbara, we understand that it is difficult for you.'

'I just feel like I shouldn't be here, not today,' she said. 'It's all wrong and not comfortable for any of us.' Barbara was surprised to find she was crying as she finished speaking. Zeliha took her hand.

'Do not worry. It has been a long day for you. If you like, you can go to the bedroom, and have your tea in peace? Or I will sit with you if you wish for company. It will be better tomorrow, you will see. You will be able to go home and you will be fine.'

'Oh Zeliha, you've been so kind to me, I'm sorry not to be more sociable, after your hospitality but that would be best, I think. I'd like to just be quiet now, thank you.'

The two women went upstairs, but instead of the room in which she'd slept earlier, Zeliha showed Barbara into a large, nicely-furnished bedroom, at the rear of the building, overlooking the courtyard to one side. 'This is a nice room,' said Zeliha, as she lowered the blind and switched on a small lamp beside the bed. 'It is quiet in here for you. There is a robe on the chair over there you are welcome to wear. Please call me if you need anything, OK?'

Barbara thanked her again, and when Zeliha had gone, she placed her mug of tea on the bedside table, undressed quickly, and wearing Zeliha's towelling bathrobe, she sat on the bed, her knees tucked up to her chest, drinking her tea and feeling calmer. She could hear the men's now-quietened voices from the courtyard. She thought she could distinguish Şerif's voice, but wasn't sure. Certainly no-one sounded as raucous as he had been earlier, during the meal. She remembered Zeliha saying that Yaman was going to speak to Şerif, and wondered what he had said, if he had done so. She felt awkward—she appreciated Yaman's thoughtfulness but really, didn't Şerif have every right to feel happy that his sister had had her baby?

She looked around the room. Kilims in rich colours were hung on three of the walls, along the other was a low chaise-type seat, with tapestry cushions stacked along the back and a towel folded on the seat. Next to that was a small dressing table and mirror, a chair in front of it. She rummaged in her bag for the things she had bought at the shop and used earlier, to freshen up; a toothbrush and paste, a bar of oatmeal soap, a face flannel, a small bottle of moisturiser. She picked up the towel and went to the bathroom. Refreshed after a wash, she returned to her room and although she thought she would lay awake mulling things over in the unfamiliar surroundings, she quickly fell asleep, without putting out the light.

TWENTY FIVE

She had woken early next morning, and found Zeliha in the kitchen with the baby. Barbara made tea for herself and the two women chatted quietly, fussing over the little boy. Barbara assumed that Şerif was still sleeping, in another room, but Zeliha told her that he had stayed the night with other friends of his who lived nearby, as Barbara had slept in the room he was using.

When he arrived, just after ten o'clock, Barbara was ready and eager to leave, although she hoped this was not too obvious to Zeliha and Yaman, who had been kind hosts. She thanked them for their hospitality, promised to call on them if she was in London, and then she and Şerif made their way by tube across to Marble Arch from where she could get the bus to Oxford.

'I'm sorry I took over your room last night,' Barbara said as they walked to the tube station.

'It is no problem,' Şerif replied, 'I have many places I can stay here, I know many people—friends who know my family.'

'Well, thank you, anyway. And for coming with me this morning, there's really no need, you know?'

'There is need—I must make sure that you are OK, I promised Mehmet. And I want to say sorry if I upset you last night.'

'You promised . . . What? When will you guys get it into your heads that I am all right, and I don't need 'looking after'? I'm not about to rush out and 'top myself' just because something I knew was going to happen, happened, OK?' She realised that Şerif had not understood all of what she'd said, for he stopped walking and just stood there, staring down at the pavement. Barbara felt sorry for berating him and turned back. She touched his arm.

'Oh look, I'm sorry,' she said. 'It's all been a bit strange, that's all. And you don't have to apologise, not really. I just shouldn't have been here when you wanted to celebrate your sister's news.'

Şerif looked at her and then down again. 'It is because . . .' he hesitated. 'When you said you were all right about the baby, and you said you did not think of Mehmet like a lover any more . . .'

'What?'

'I hear this and I am happy. I think that maybe you will see me as a boyfriend, if we like each other. Then I am stupid and drink too much—no, it is true—Yaman told me I was not being polite and I had upset you. I am sorry, Barbara.'

Barbara took her hand from Şerif's arm. 'But Şerif, I had no idea that you thought like that,' she said. 'I probably wouldn't have come to meet you if I had known. I wouldn't have wanted to encourage you. I'm sorry, but right now I don't want a relationship—a boyfriend—at all. I've too much to do at work, and . . . well, I just don't want to, OK? Sorry. Please—let's not talk about it again.'

And Şerif had not spoken about it again. Throughout their journey, he hadn't said much at all, just passing the occasional comment on places they passed through. He seemed positively sullen by the time they arrived at the Oxford bus stop. Barbara felt impatient, she couldn't be doing with this; all she wanted was to get home. She was relieved to see the bus coming, and as it stopped and its doors opened, she gave Şerif a peck on the cheek, said she hoped he would enjoy the rest of his holiday, and climbed aboard, choosing a seat on the far side, away from the pavement and Hyde Park—away from Şerif. But she needn't have worried; he was no longer there, he didn't wait for the bus to leave.

The first thing Barbara did when she got back to her flat at lunch-time was to have a long shower and wash her hair. That done, she made herself a large mug of tea and took it out into the garden where she sat at her large wooden garden table and lit a cigarette. As soon as she had arrived home, her head felt lighter, somehow; she felt relieved to be back among her own things and alone.

The light was flashing on her answer-phone, but when she played it, no-one spoke, all she heard was a few clicks before the line went dead. She wondered if it was Şerif, or maybe Mehmet, but couldn't be bothered to think much about it. She had had enough of everything to do with them for the moment. The phone rang while she was still standing next to it and made her jump.

'Hello?'

'Hello Barbara, it's me, Sean, how are you?'

'Oh Sean, hello, it's lovely to hear from you. I'm OK, thanks, I've just got back from London and . . .' she couldn't say more as she felt choked.

'You still there?' Sean asked.

'Oh god it was awful,' Barbara sobbed into the phone. 'I'm sorry, I'll be all right in a minute.'

'Barbara, whatever's wrong? What's happened?'

Barbara took a deep breath and managed to tell him about her trip to London, about being ill, and the news of Mehmet's baby. As usual, he let her talk, uninterrupted, until she reached the end of her story.

'Ach, love, no wonder you're feeling rough,' he said softly. 'Why not go round to Rosalind and Mags? They'll look after you. Wish I was there to do so myself.'

'Thanks. And that's sweet of you. I might well go round later. Right now I think I'll have a sleep. It's really warm here but I feel cold.'

'Probably the stress of the last couple of days. Look, I'll let you get off to your bed and I'll ring you tonight, OK? You sure you'll be all right?'

'Yes, sorry I laid all that on you. I'm sure you weren't expecting a neurotic wreck to answer the phone! I was so glad to hear your voice and it just all came out. What about you—are you OK? By the way, did you call earlier? There was a 'non-message' on the answerphone.'

'No, it wasn't me. Don't worry, you're just tired and wound up.

We'll have a proper talk tonight, but I'm grand, everything's fine here. Now, go for your nap. 'Bye.'

Barbara went to bed and laid there feeling calmer. She was sure that her reaction would have been the same if Rosalind or Mags had called. It was the relief of being able to 'let go', with those who are close to us; not having to keep up a facade of being in control. All the same, she was pleased that it was Sean who had called her. She pulled the duvet up to her neck and drifted off to sleep feeling warm and comfortable at last. She woke at four, feeling much better. She walked round to Rosalind and Mags' house, but unusually, there was no-one in. Returning home, she decided to make dinner for herself and also to make a cake to take into work for her colleagues next day. By seven-thirty, there was a fruit cake sitting on a cooling rack in the kitchen, and Barbara sat down to her meal of chicken Caesar salad with warm new potatoes. She felt that enough time had passed since 'the *raki* episode' to be safely over the 'I'll never touch alcohol again' stage that often follows having drunk too much, so she opened a bottle of Bordeaux and had a glass with her dinner.

Good as his word, Sean rang back just before nine. They talked for over an hour, about what each had been up to since they last spoke. Barbara was again pleased to hear Sean so animated and enthusiastic about his job and his house. He asked her about her plans for the coming months, and she had to admit that she hadn't made, or even thought about making, any plans at all. 'I guess you could say that I've been 'going with the flow,' she said, smiling as she remembered Rosalind's advice to her.

'So you've no holidays planned then?' Sean asked her.

'Well, no. Haven't thought about it. Work's been a bit odd lately; there's the big 'restructuring' of the whole organisation coming up, and that might mean that my job changes quite a lot. I won't be travelling for work much in the future, it seems.'

'Will you mind that?'

'I'd rather that travelling *was* part of the job, but I've done such a lot of it over the last couple of years that I wouldn't mind a rest from it. But morale in the office isn't good at the moment, everyone feels

133

in limbo about what's happening to their jobs, their departments, it's all unsettling. And meanwhile, the situation in Bosnia and Serbia is still dreadful—you'd think the organisation would have enough to think about without "internal politics".'

'You sound like you could do with a break—why not come over here for a while? You're always welcome.'

'Oh Sean that's a lovely idea, I'll have a think about it—see when I can take some leave from work. Is there anytime that's best for you? Will you be able to have time off if I come to see you?'

'Sure, that won't be a problem. I hope you'll come, I think you'd like it here.'

And so it was that by the end of their conversation, Barbara felt excited about going into work the next day to check the leave calendar and to begin making plans for her holiday in Ireland, with Sean.

TWENTY SIX

It turned out that Barbara had a considerable amount of leave which needed to be taken before the end of the year, and no-one at work raised any objection to her booking three weeks off at the end of September. She phoned Sean with the news that she had done so, and began checking out flights. Sean now called several times a week, always with more ideas for what they might do and places they would go to when she was with him.

She also received a letter from Mehmet, in which she learned that Gul and the baby were going to join him in the middle of August. He also said that he had phoned her the day she got back from London, but that when he got the answerphone, he couldn't think what to say, so didn't leave a message. Barbara got the distinct impression that it was because he had assumed she was staying in London with Şerif until late, and was 'narked' about it. The rest of his letter sounded 'sulky', somehow, with a definite air of self-pity, very unlike Mehmet. Barbara sent a card in reply, simply congratulating him on the arrival of the baby, and hoping that they would quickly find somewhere suitable to live.

During August, Samira, from Azerbaijan, came to Oxford for a fortnight for a conference. Barbara was pleased to be able to return the hospitality that had been shown to her in Baku and they spent several enjoyable evenings having pub meals, and even went to a folk club session which Samira enjoyed immensely. When Barbara told her that her 'friend' in Baku was preparing for the arrival of his girlfriend and their baby, Samira immediately offered to take any gifts back with her if Barbara wanted to send anything. So one afternoon, Barbara took time off to go shopping with Mags, for baby clothes; an unusual experience for them both. They arrived back to show Rosalind what they had bought.

'Isn't this too sweet?' said Mags, holding up a denim dungaree set with stripey t-shirt. 'And look what we've got here,' she showed Rosalind a soft, red, toy elephant and a pair of bright blue pull-on bootees.

'I can see that you've had fun,' said Rosalind, picking up the elephant and laughing. 'It's good of Samira to take these things back with her. Barbara, can I talk to you a moment? Shall we go into the dining room?'

As Barbara followed Rosalind into the other room, she was surprised to see her wink at Mags. 'What's up?' she asked.

'Oh nothing's wrong, dear,' Rosalind replied. 'It's an idea I've had that I want to run by you, that's all. I'd like to help Mehmet, too, but the best thing I think I can do is to send him some money. Do you think that it would be all right to do that? I know how proud these young men are, and I don't want him to feel awkward about it. What do you think?'

'Well I think you're right about the pride thing, but if you were to send it back with Samira if that's OK with her, I don't know if there's a limit on how much she can take into the country, how much were you thinking of sending?'

'I thought five hundred pounds.'

'That's quite a large sum. It would go a long way in Azerbaijan.'

'But do you think he will accept it? I don't want him to feel insulted or anything.'

'Why not speak to Samira and ask her advice about the money? I mean, she'll know about banks and other types of accounts won't she? If she could take the money—a cheque maybe—open an account for him with it, then we just tell him it's a collection we had which is in the account for his use. Then we get Samira to give him the account details .It's only a small lie, but I think he's likely to be less uncomfortable with that than if he thought it was all coming from one person, I don't know why.'

'I think I know what you mean, dear. And it's a good idea to speak to Samira. Let's ask her to supper again on Thursday evening and I'll talk to her then.'

'Does Mags know about your idea to send money?' Barbara asked, half smiling.

'Of course, why do you ask?'

'Because I saw you winking at her as we left the room, so I knew you were planning something!' she laughed.

Samira thought that Barbara's idea of setting up an account was indeed the best way to get the money to Mehmet, so on the night before she left for Baku, they all had supper together and she and Rosalind spent some time going through the details. She left in a taxi with all the necessary paperwork for the transaction, and with the brightly-wrapped gifts for the baby. Barbara immediately posted off another card to Mehmet, giving him Samira's telephone number, along with the contact details of the office in Baku, and asking him to get in touch with Samira as soon as possible, as he needed to collect gifts from them—she didn't mention anything about the money, thinking that was best left until Samira had set up the account.

Barbara now felt 'freed' from having to worry about Mehmet. She felt guilty about this at first, as she believed that he had genuinely been in love with her, and it was only a moment of stupidity that had resulted in Gul's pregnancy. If not for that—well, who knew what might have become of her relationship with him? But since she had returned from Azerbaijan, she knew that her feelings had changed towards him, and she was sure this was true of his for her, also.

She was enjoying the summer in Oxford. She loved her flat and the garden. One of her great pleasures was to have friends round for meals and to eat outside. Barbara had created a lovely relaxing space in her garden, which was quite magical once it grew dark, as she had secreted lamps and candles all over the place, which twinkled and glowed among the plants. 'It's just like Fairyland!', one of her friends had exclaimed one evening, and Barbara felt no shame at all in the pride she felt on hearing this.

Samira sent Barbara a fax soon after she returned to Baku to say that she had made contact with Mehmet—the two of them had met for coffee. She said that Mehmet had been surprised about the bank account she had set up for him, but after initial embarrassment, and following Samira's assurances that it was a perfectly sensible arrangement, he gratefully agreed to accept the money 'collected', as he believed, by his friends in Oxford.

Shortly after this, Barbara received a beautifully embroidered card from Mehmet, thanking her, Rosalind and Mags for their generosity, and said that it would make a big difference to getting the baby 'settled' when Gul arrived with him in Baku. Barbara felt relieved. It was a chatty note from Mehmet; he sounded more relaxed, and she was pleased that Rosalind's plan had worked out so well.

Of course, at that time she had no way of knowing how very different she would feel the next time she heard from Mehmet and how many things would change in so many people's lives afterwards.

TWENTY SEVEN

September 1995

'Barbara? It is Şerif here, in Istanbul. I must speak with you. I will call again. OK?'

Barbara played the answerphone message again but still couldn't get a clue about why Şerif had called or why he sounded so anxious.

Mags was with her when she got in from work and played the message.

'Well, he sounds a bit . . . strange,' she said to Barbara. 'Is that the first you've heard from him since you were in London?'

'Yes. To be honest, I didn't expect to hear from him again! I wonder what's prompted him to call me now?'

'Maybe he's coming back to London for another visit and wants to see you again—give it another go, you know?'

'I bloody well hope not!' said Barbara, 'I'm pretty sure he got the message when I told him I wasn't interested. I'll just have to see if he calls back, I guess.'

'Sod's Law says that he'll call back when we're out tonight,' said Mags.

'Probably, but it can't be helped. I'll just change my clothes and we'll go and meet the others.'

They were going to see 'Jules et Jim'—part of the Truffaut season running at the cinema in Walton Street, with some of Barbara's colleagues. Rosalind had seen the film 'countless times', she'd said, and had work to do earlier in the evening, so arranged to meet them after the film for a drink. Being a huge Truffaut fan herself, it was the third time that Barbara had seen the film, but enjoyed it all the same. While watching the film, with its 'three-way relationship' plot, she found herself thinking about Mehmet, Sean, and even Şerif; and of how strange are the ways our lives lead us.

They'd had a couple of drinks with Rosalind in The Jericho Tavern, and it was late when Barbara left Mags and Rosalind at the end of her street after walking back along the Banbury Road together.

She let herself in and noticed straight away that the answerphone light was blinking. She hung up her jacket and bag and pressed 'Play'.

'Barbara? This is Mehmet. There is an accident . . . was accident I mean. The metro. Oh I do not know how to say . . . in the fire . . . they say many people are down there. Gul is not home since yesterday. We think she is in accident . . . this is big worry for us. Şerif is coming here tonight from Istanbul. I will try to call you tomorrow . . .'

Barbara sat on the floor and played the message again. And then a third time. The back of her scalp felt prickly and her thoughts were racing. Although it was late, she called Rosalind and Mags' number. Rosalind answered.

'Sorry it's late, it's me,'

'Hello dear, what's the matter?'

'I've had the most awful message from Mehmet—he's worried sick. Gul—you know—the baby's mother? She's missing and there's been an accident of some sort in the Metro in Baku. He said a fire. I don't know if the baby is with her too . . . oh that's just too awful.'

'Oh how dreadful,' replied Rosalind. 'Just a second, Barbara, I'm just going to tell Mags, she's wondering what's up.'

Barbara heard her tell Mags what had happened.

'Do you have a number for Mehmet in Baku? I don't think you have, have you?' Rosalind asked.

'No. He said he'd try to call me again tomorrow. This could explain why Şerif called me earlier—in fact, I'm sure that was it. I don't know what to do.'

'There's nothing any of us can do tonight, dear. Let's all sleep on it and work something out tomorrow. At least it's Saturday tomorrow and we can get together—would you like to come round first thing for breakfast and we'll talk then?'

'Thanks, yes, that would be good. I don't think I'll sleep much, but you're right, we can't do anything tonight. I'll see you in the morning, 'night.'

Barbara was right about not sleeping. She felt it would be wrong, somehow, to just go to bed when Mehmet and those around him were having such a bad time. Instead, she paced around the flat, drinking tea and smoking cigarettes in the early hours, and thinking, thinking, thinking.

She realised she had 'been here before'—trying to get in touch with Mehmet in Baku, but even when she remembered that it was Osman who had helped last time, and would in all likelihood do so again, she knew she couldn't very well call The Meydan at this hour.

She must have fallen asleep on the sofa sometime after five, which was the last time she could remember looking at her watch. It was now a bit before seven and she felt stiff and chilly. A half-full mug of cold tea was beside her on the table, along with an over-full ashtray and several photo albums from her visit to Istanbul the year before. She'd looked through the photos during the night, thinking how long ago it seemed and how much had changed since that time. There they were: Mehmet; Osman; the hotel in the aftermath of the storm; the Princes' Islands; even some of Rosalind and Mags. Sitting up, she spotted the albums and leant forward, placing her hand on top of the uppermost album, her eyes filled with tears. She shook her head and took several deep breaths. *'Come on, get yourself together girl, tears won't help,'* she told herself and shuffled off for a shower.

By nine o'clock, Barbara was seated at the kitchen table at Lonsdale Rd; Mags held Barbara's hand between her own while Barbara told them that she thought she should go out to Baku—not that she knew what she could do once there. Rosalind poured coffee for them: 'I can understand that you feel you have to help him, dear, we all do, but I just don't think that going out there is the right thing—certainly not at the moment.'

'Probably right, but I just can't stand this 'not knowing'—I thought about calling Osman at the hotel, he knows Gul's family and has the number for Mehmet in Baku. But if he hasn't heard about the accident I don't want to be the one to tell him.'

'Why don't I call the hotel?' Rosalind got up and fetched a notepad and pen from the dresser. 'At least I can speak to whoever answers in their own language and I might be able to find out something, even if Osman isn't there. Now, let's write some things down so I've got a crib sheet when I'm on the phone.'

So with her notes, Rosalind went out to the phone in the hall and dialled the hotel, Barbara and Mags dragged out three chairs from the kitchen and they sat grouped around the telephone.

Rosalind spoke in rapid, fluent Turkish, then turned to them 'Osman is there, they've gone to get him.' She spoke into the phone again for several minutes, by her tone, it was obvious to Barbara and Mags that Osman already knew what had happened in Baku. She turned to Barbara: 'He'd like to speak to you, is that OK?'

'Of course. He knows, doesn't he?'

Rosalind nodded and handed her the phone. 'Osman? Hello I hope you don't mind us calling you but we're so worried. Isn't it dreadful? Have you spoken to Mehmet? Do they have any news yet?'

Poor Osman, the bombardment of questions in English threw him a bit, after talking with Rosalind in Turkish.

'Hello Barbara. Yes, it is bad. I am with Şerif yesterday and he told me . . . the fire in the train. He is gone now to Baku. I call Mehmet tonight when Şerif is there.'

'OK, Osman, would you be able to call us when you have spoken to them—to let us know what's happening? Şerif and Mehmet called me last night but I wasn't at home, they left messages. Oh it's so awful, the poor girl. And the baby, I just . . .'

'Not baby.'

'What?'

'Not baby, he is with Mehmet at the house. Gul's brother's wife is looking after him.'

'So Gul was on her own?'

'Yes, she went to shops. I will call you at the lady's house tonight, yes?'

'Yes, please. That's so kind, Osman, thank you. Don't worry Mehmet about calling us, he's got enough to think about, but when you speak to him, tell him . . .' ('*Tell him what?*' She thought, '*what can I possibly say to him?*')

'Tell him I'm sorry I wasn't at home when he called and . . . and I'm thinking of them all.'

'I will do that, do not worry, I will find out news and call tonight.'

'Thanks. Rosalind will speak to you now and give you the number, OK?' She passed the phone back to Rosalind and turned to Mags.

'The baby's all right, he wasn't with her. She had just gone shopping when it happened, it seems, poor girl.'

'We don't know what's happened to her yet. She might be all right—well, she may not be . . .' Mag's voice trailed off. 'She could be injured and trapped there, or at a hospital—you know how chaotic these things are. She might be all right.'

'I wish I could believe that, but I fear for her . . . for all of them.'

Rosalind finished speaking and replaced the receiver. 'He's going to ring here at nine o'clock,' she said. 'Now all we can do is wait.'

TWENTY EIGHT

'Hey, love, slow down now, you're awful upset, obviously. This all happened yesterday?' Sean had been surprised to get a call so early from Barbara, and was trying to make sense of what she was telling him.

'I'm sorry . . . sorry. I just wanted to let you know. Shit, it's only seven. Didn't realise the time. Look, shall I call you later? I'm sorry, I . . .'

'Will you stop apologising? It's OK. So they're sure the poor girl's died are they?'

'It seems so. Osman said that her brothers had gone to the hospital with Mehmet and then had called her parents in Istanbul—to break the news, I guess. Oh Sean, it was so strange when Rosalind was on the phone to him yesterday, in the morning, I mean. She kept saying 'Ateş . . . Ateş', so I thought the baby had died too . . . his name, y'know? It means 'Fire' but they use it to mean 'blaze' or that kind of thing, so they weren't talking about him at all, just about the accident.'

'Ach, it's dreadful. It was on the radio news last night—they said it was the worst subway fire ever. Sure you don't know whether to feel glad or sorry that the little one is OK. Christ—that's awful to say, of course it's good that he survived but, oh I don't know what I'm saying really.'

'It's OK, I know what you mean. Osman said that he's all right—the baby—he's used to being with his auntie and her kids. It's Mehmet

144

I'm worried most about. I keep wondering if I should go out there to help him in some way, but that's probably not a good idea.'

'I don't think it's the place for you at the moment, love. Think about it—it's going to be a family time for them; a bereavement of any kind is a family thing, but this sort of tragedy . . . well, even more so. I know you want to help, it's in your nature, and I know it's difficult to think of it all going on somewhere far away.'

'Hmm . . . that's exactly what Rosalind said. You two often come out with the same lines, y'know? As for it being 'in my nature', I always thought it was a good thing, a positive one, to want to help and to be kind, although it seems not everyone thinks so.'

'What do you mean? It is good, 'course it is. Who's told you it's not?'

'Oh, one of the new managers at work. Said to someone—another colleague, but one close to me—that I always seemed to be getting 'too involved' in other people's lives.'

'Why would she say that?'

'Well, it was when I wanted a day off because I was doing the food and reading something at a friend's husband's funeral—back in June. Jenny's husband, do you remember I told you about it?'

'Yes, so you did. But that's just unfair— and unkind, too. No-one has any right to decide when and who you get 'involved' with, if that's the word. Silly cow!'

Barbara was taken aback by this—Sean didn't usually come out with that sort of comment, certainly not about people he hadn't met.

'Aye well, people are strange, I guess.' Barbara said, wanting to change the subject. More and more, lately, she found herself thinking how unsettled she felt at work, but she didn't want to think about all that now, not with all the emotional hoo-ha going on in Baku—and in her head.

'Do you think I should still come to see you? I mean, it's only a couple of weeks' time, isn't it? I don't know if . . .'

'Why wouldn't you come?' Sean cut in. 'Because of what's going on with Mehmet, you mean?'

'Well, yes, I guess that's what I meant, but I don't know. It seems wrong to be taking myself off on holiday when . . . I mean, to some-where that he can't . . .'

'You're worried that Mehmet will want to get in touch with you while you're at mine? Sure, you can give him my number and what difference does it make where you're speaking to him from?

'Oh Sean, why do you always see through the crap to simple solutions? You really wouldn't mind if he rang when I was with you?'

'Look—you had a relationship, of whatever kind and for however long, with this guy. You're friends with him. And with what he's going through at the moment, I think the poor guy deserves the help of all the friends he can get, don't you? And who am I to have any say in who you speak to or think about any time—even when you're staying with me? That's weirdly possessive and you know that's not 'me'—don't you?'

'Yes, sorry, I guess it's not as if we're . . .'

'We're what? Not 'an item', were you going to say? 'Involved'? Listen, even if we were—and you never know we could be one day, 'Barbara felt herself blush when he came out with this, and she had to force herself to concentrate on what Sean was continuing to say.

'. . . it wouldn't be any different. I hope you don't think I'm just after a wee wifey to lock away in the kitchen and take care of me for the rest of her days?'

Barbara laughed, but she felt embarrassed and annoyed that she'd steered the conversation in this direction without meaning to.

'Of course I don't! I just don't expect anyone to accept—well, the 'baggage' that comes with me, I suppose.'

'But we all have baggage. We'd be dull creatures if we didn't, at our age, so.'

'There you go again! Rosalind said almost exactly the same to me, a while ago, when we were talking about . . . well, people and stuff.'

She knew very well that it had been when Mags had been teasing her one day about Sean and where their relationship might go, that she'd talked to her and to Rosalind about 'baggage' and past histo-ries, but she stopped herself saying this to Sean—she didn't want

146

to go there right now, although their conversation seemed to keep 'going there' of its own accord.

'People and stuff, eh? She's a good woman to talk with about 'people and stuff'! But listen, I have to go to Belfast this morning, so I'm going to have to get on. Shall I call you tonight?'

'That would be great—if you can. Sorry I called so early.'

'It's not a problem, honestly. I'll call about nine, OK? Oh, and Barbara—I really hope you will come, I'll be sad if you don't. Cheers, now, 'bye.'

She couldn't help smiling as she hung up. She was pleased that Sean was so keen on her visit, and he always was able to make her feel better. Pottering around the flat, she thought more about Sean: after the 'London and Şerif' fiasco and now the news of Gul's death, she realised that Sean had 'been there' for her—he'd been the obvious one she needed to speak to on both occasions. Was she beginning to rely on him, and if so, was that a bad thing? Whenever she began to think like this, considering the 'ifs and buts', it would always come back to remembering Rosalind's advice to 'go with the flow' (and yes, of course, Sean's advice had been the same). She'd heard the new single from *Oasis* recently—*Roll with it*—and thought how it spoke to her, right now. It had all the makings of a classic with a high position in her own personal Top Twenty. Deciding that she'd buy the CD for Sean and take it with her to give to him, she realised that she'd banished thoughts of not going to Ireland and was most definitely looking forward to seeing him again.

TWENTY NINE

At a certain point during the flight to Ireland they announced that it is possible to see both Ireland and England out of the window as the plane crosses the Irish Sea. Barbara loved this spectacle, it made Ireland and all things Irish seem closer to her 'normal life', somehow. When the announcement came, she pressed her head against the window and gazed at the view far below. She thought about other journeys she'd made during the last couple of years, realising that the thing that made this flight very different to all the others was that it was of such short duration. '*Barely enough time to get settled in the seat before you're landing again,*' she thought. Sure enough, the descent began. She fastened her tray-table back up to the seat in front and returned her book to her bag.

Sean was to meet her at Belfast International Airport. He'd been working frequently in Belfast and would meet Barbara on his way home, he'd said, after spending the week in the city. He lived near Loughanure in the heart of the Gaeltacht area of Donegal, and Barbara had looked at maps and guidebooks almost every night before she left—'swotting up' on the area.

She'd spoken to Mehmet twice on the phone following the accident. He'd sounded distant. 'Not in miles,' she'd said to Rosalind and Mags, '. . . in his mind, I mean. He sounds so . . . well, stunned by it all.'

'Hardly surprising, given what he's been through,' Mags had replied.

'The awful thing is that he's blaming himself for Gul even being in Baku at that time,' Barbara explained. 'I tried to tell him that she could easily have been there visiting her brother and could have been involved in the accident—or any accident at any time—even if she'd never met Mehmet, but he feels responsible, it's obvious by the way he's talking.'

'Is he all right to remain there, with her family? Rosalind asked. 'He still can't go back to Turkey can he, if he wants to avoid his National Service?'

'From what he said, Gul's death has brought him closer to her family, thank goodness. Her sister-in-law will continue to look after Ateş, and Mehmet can continue working at the casino. He'd just found a small flat to rent, for the three of them, but now he's going to stay with Gul's brother and his family to be with the baby as much as possible. He's not making any other plans yet, which is probably for the best.'

Barbara at least felt relieved to have spoken to Mehmet before she left for Ireland and had given him Sean's number so that he could call her there in the three weeks she'd be away if he wanted to. She'd also given Rosalind and Mags Sean's number and also the number in Belfast where he would be until he met her at the airport. Mags had told her to 'stop fussing' when she did so, which made Barbara laugh—she didn't think she was a 'fussing' sort, really.

As the plane descended, Barbara smiled as she thought of Rosalind and Mags and how they hadn't been able to hide their delight that she was to visit Sean. 'For goodness sake, you two,' Barbara had said to them only that morning as they sat in the kitchen at Lonsdale Road. 'You're like a couple of Indian 'aunties' packing me off to get married! Will you stop fussing so?'

Patting Barbara's shoulder as she passed behind her chair to put the kettle on, Rosalind had replied 'Well, you never know, dear, one can but hope!'

They drove in Rosalind's car to the bus station at Gloucester Green for Barbara to get the bus to Heathrow. They had offered to drive her to the airport, but Barbara was used to leaving on her travels on the bus, so had preferred it this way. As Mags was taking bags out of the boot, Rosalind had given Barbara a tiny felt leprechaun as a 'travel mascot' and, holding Barbara's shoulders, she had kissed the top of her head in farewell. The bus pulled out, and Barbara waved fondly at the two of them; these unconventional women who had become such dear friends in such a short time; as they stood waving back and blowing kisses.

It was obvious that Rosalind and Mags thought Sean would be an ideal partner for her, but Barbara felt slightly uncomfortable about their teasing. Hadn't she embarrassed herself enough that time when she'd assumed he'd wanted to stay the night with her? What if he didn't want 'that' type of relationship? Then again, he'd himself hinted at the prospect of a future relationship hadn't he? She stopped her musings with a shake of the head and concentrated on the plane landing and on getting herself into the baggage hall without the butterflies in her stomach distracting her too much.

Before heading to collect her bag, she'd dived into the ladies' loo and re-applied her eye-liner and run her hands through her hair. Now, standing at the luggage carousel, Barbara smiled every time there was an announcement—she loved the accents.

Suddenly, it crept into her consciousness that the announcement was for her . . . *'Would Barbara Anderson, Barbara Anderson, arriving on flight number . . .'* She spun round, missing the rest of the announcement.

'That's me,' she blurted out as she bumped against the man standing behind her.

'Excuse me, oh, sorry, I'm . . .' She felt hemmed in by all the other passengers waiting there and unable to get clear of the tangle of legs, feet and trolleys. Then she heard it again: *'. . . go to the Information Desk immediately.'*

She found herself 'spat out' of the crowd as though from a rugby scrum, and stood there for a moment, not knowing what to do. She'd yet to retrieve her bag, but should she go to the Information Desk first? *'Probably just Sean letting me know where he'll meet me,'* she thought. But she knew it was highly unlikely that he'd be able to get an 'APB' announcement made just for that. She began to feel bad: a creeping dread at the back of her neck.

'Are you all right, miss?' A Customs officer touched her arm, his face showing concern.

'Oh, yes . . . I mean, no, not really—the announcement—it's me. It's me they want. I'm to go to Information, but I have to get my bag . . .'

'That's all right, miss, I'll take you there and we'll get your bag. Come on, now. I'm Michael by the way.' Barbara allowed herself to be led out of the baggage hall, stopping to describe her bag and give her details to one of Michael's female colleagues. 'Sure that's no problem,' the woman had said. 'We'll get your bag to Information just now.'

'Barbara! Barbara—over here!'

She looked over in the direction of the voice. Sean was waving his arms at them from the other side of a taped-off area. 'I'll see you at Information,' he shouted, pointing to the Information Desk sign.

Next thing, Sean was in front of her; his arms around her. Barbara sank against his chest as he thanked Michael for his help.

'Sean, what's happening? Is everything all right?' she asked him without moving her head.

Sean held her arms and gently moved her away from him. Looking into her eyes, as if explaining to a child, he said: 'We're going into the room at the back there, behind the Information Desk. They'll bring your bag. We'll get a cup of tea.'

'Will you just tell me what's wrong?' Barbara was flushed, not used to others taking control.

'Not here, come on with me,' and Sean took her arm, leading her to a door held open by an airport official.

Once they were seated on a narrow couch, Sean took Barbara's hands in his and began: 'I had a phone call this afternoon . . .'

'Who from? Is it Mehmet? What's happened now?'

'Shhhh, wait now. No, it's not Mehmet. It was Gareth.'

'Gareth? As in my 'ex' Gareth? What the hell? Why was . . . How did he . . . Oh Sean what's happened?'

'I'm afraid it's Rosalind,' he said. They'd just got back from taking you to the bus. She collapsed in the garden at Lonsdale Road. Mags called an ambulance but . . .'

'What? She's OK isn't she? Oh love, tell me she's OK.'

'She had gone by the time the ambulance got to the hospital. It was a heart attack, it seems.'

'Nooooooooo!' Barbara let out a long cry, rocking forward over her knees. Sean rubbed and patted her back.

'There now,' he soothed. 'There now.'

After several long minutes, taking a deep breath, Barbara sat up, her words came in sobs: 'What . . . about . . . Mags? Oh Christ—where . . . is . . . she?'

'She went to the hospital—she's in such a state that they contacted the University and somehow your ex ended up there with her, along with a couple more of their friends. They all took her back to the house, and the wife of one of the tutors is looking after her. She's sedated now, but she kept talking about you and letting you know. That's why Gareth called me—Mags gave the number to them at the house.'

Barbara didn't seem to be listening. She was rocking backwards and forwards, her duffle bag on her lap. She was holding something in her hands, touching it gently with her fingers.

'Here's some tea for us now,' Sean got up to take the tray from a woman as she came through the door.

'What's that you've got there?' he asked Barbara, squatting in front of her. Barbara's turned her tear-stained face towards him. She held up the tiny leprechaun toy. 'From her this morning,' she whispered, before her body again convulsed in soundless grief.

THIRTY

The following hours passed in a blur as far as Barbara was concerned. Even before she arrived, Sean had booked them on a flight back to Heathrow that evening and had also arranged to pick up a hire car at the airport. He rang the house in Lonsdale Road to let people there know that he and Barbara were coming back straight away. He'd asked if she wanted to speak to anyone on the phone, but Barbara just shook her head, numbing shock making her incapable of any kind of decision. All she could do was to follow Sean's gentle instructions to 'wait there', 'sit here' and so on, until she 'came to' a little to find herself once again leaning her forehead against the aircraft window, staring at lights far below.

'What are we going to do?' She said, without moving and to no-one in particular.

Sean turned to her, leant his head close to hers. 'We're going to go back to Oxford, love. We can go to your place or straight to see Mags, whichever you'd rather.'

'I don't know. I was meaning rather: 'What are we going to do without Rosalind?' What's going to happen?'

'Sure it's only just happened and all we can do at the moment is to comfort one another. Don't worry about anything else for now.'

It was gone midnight when they landed. Sean called the house and was told that Mags was sleeping, so decided for them that they would go to Barbara's flat until the morning. Barbara was obviously in shock; when they arrived home, she wandered around, touching things; still wearing her jacket and clutching the toy leprechaun. Sean let her be. He made tea, found some brandy in the kitchen cupboard, and took it all on a tray into the sitting room. Barbara had opened the doors to the garden and gone outside. He leant down and switched on the garden lights—creating the 'fairyland' that Barbara loved so much. She turned to face him and he could see she was crying.

'Sean, thank you for making it beautiful,' she said, tears rolling down her face.

He put his arms around her and let her cry.

Many mugs of tea and a few brandies helped pass the hours until at last Barbara fell asleep on the sofa. There had been little conversation between them; Sean offering reassurance as best he could to Barbara's occasional questions and worries. Now that she slept, he took the duvet from her bed, covered her with it, and himself went into the garden; it was already dawn. He took one of Barbara's cigarettes and smoked it, even though he'd given up over a year before. Finally, he lay on the bed and slept, his last thoughts were of the very long, draining day they had ahead of them.

'Can't go in there.' Barbara stood at the gate of Rosalind's house. 'I . . . I just can't . . . it's not . . .' Sean moved to stand in front of her. 'Come on love, I know it's difficult, but Mags needs you and I think you need to be together. It'll be OK, I'll be with you, let's go in now.'

She allowed him to lead the way and he rang the bell. 'I usually go round to the back door, through the garden,' she said, vaguely. 'Haven't rung the bell for ages. Everything's wrong now,'

Caroline, wife of one of the Faculty tutors, answered the door and led them into the kitchen; she had been at the house all night. Barbara felt a tightness in her throat and found it hard to breathe properly. She held Sean's hand so tight that it hurt him as her nails dug in.

'I'm not sure how to do this but I know I've got to,' she whispered.

Mags was awake, Caroline told them. She had taken her some tea at six, when the first thing she'd asked was if Barbara was home yet. She was still fairly sedated—the hospital had sent them off with tablets to help her over the next few days and Caroline had administered some to her already that morning.

'Would you like to go up now?' Caroline asked. 'Or would you like some tea first—or something stronger? I know it's only eight o'clock, but by the look of the two of you I don't think it would do you any harm!'

At Sean's suggestion, they each took a small tumbler of brandy and warm water, a teaspoon of honey stirred into it. 'This was my ma's patent 'soother' at times of crisis,' he said, sipping his drink.

He noticed that Barbara's eyes were darting everywhere; as if taking in every detail of the room for the first time. She looked flushed after the brandy but he thought this was probably better than the deathly pale she had been before it.

'That was a good idea,' Barbara said as she stood and placed her empty glass on the table.

'OK, I'd better go and see her now.'

'Do you want me to come up with you?' Sean asked. 'Will she be OK with that, do you think?'

'I'd like you to be near, but I'll go in on my own. Could you come up and wait on the landing? Would that be all right?'

Sean took her hand. 'Of course it is,' he said, moving to lead her to the hallway. 'No problem at all.'

The bedroom curtains were almost closed and Barbara tried to move softly across the darkened room towards the bed. She could see that Mags' eyes were closed.

'Mags? Are you awake?' she said quietly, touching her hand.

Mags stirred, her eyes flickered open. As she focused on Barbara, recognising her, she suddenly sat bolt upright, a long cry left her: 'Ohhhhhhhhhhh!' She held out her arms and Barbara folded her in tight embrace.

Sean looked in through the open door when he heard Mags cry out and could see the two of them crying and gently rocking together; holding one another so tightly, he thought, as though to let go would be the end of all things. Hearing a noise behind him, he turned to find Caroline approaching with three mugs of tea on a tray.

'How's it going?' she asked him.

'It's just desperate—heart-wrenching—to see them like this. Christ knows how they're feeling,' he replied, Caroline noticed Sean looked tearful.

'Here,' she said, 'Have some tea. It's going to be an awfully long haul, getting through this. Do you want to take this in to them or shall I?'

'You go, but if it seems right, ask them if they want me to come in.'

Sean sat on a tattered armchair on the landing, gazing at dust particles in a shaft of light from the window above the staircase, sipping his tea. He heard the front door open and Caroline's husband, David, who had been one of Sean's tutors, called 'Hello?'

'Up here,' Sean replied, leaning over the balustrade. The two men shook hands and greeted each other on the landing.

'Horrible business,' said David. 'So unexpected, you know? I fear for Margaret, it was always Rosalind who . . . well, who 'organised' everything. Seemed to be in charge always. That poor woman is going to need a lot of help get through all of this. Rosalind has no family that any of us knows of, so we're assuming that it will be down to Margaret to make arrangements . . . the funeral and all the . . . well, all the stuff one has to do after a death.'

'I don't suppose you've had a chance to speak to her about any of that?' Sean asked him.

'No, not at all. She was in no state for conversation of any sort yesterday, and I don't expect she'll be much better today, really.' David ran his hand along the banister rail as he spoke.

'But I'm going to the Faculty Office this morning, I've arranged to meet the Administrator there—good of her to come out on a Saturday. Maybe we can find out something of use in the staff records there.'

Caroline came out of the bedroom. 'Hello dear,' she said to her husband, and turning to Sean, said: 'They'd like you to go in—if you want to.'

'OK, thanks,' he said, rather awkwardly handing her his half-empty mug. He shook David's hand again.

'Good to see you, David, though I wish it weren't in these

circumstances. Can we talk later, when you've been to the office? I'll tell Barbara that you're trying to find out what you can.'

'Yes, good idea,' David replied. 'I'll come back here this afternoon, say three o'clock?'

'I'll make us something to eat—and yet more tea,' Caroline smiled as she and David turned to go. 'I'll be only downstairs if you need me, Sean. Just call.'

When he entered the room, he was surprised to see Mags smile at him. She patted the bed. 'Sean. Come and sit with us,' she said in a very quiet voice.

He stroked Barbara's shoulder as he walked round to the other side of the bed and perched on it. He leant down and kissed the top of Mags' head and took her hand.

'I'm so very, very sorry,' he said.

Mags took a deep breath. 'I know,' she said as she exhaled. 'I know, I know. But we will get through this. Barbara's told me that we'll be all right and I believe her. You used to say that to us, didn't you?' She took Barbara's hand. 'Do you remember? You said you'd always be all right because you always were, in the end.'

'That's right, love,' Barbara said, staring at their hands. 'But I've never before had such need to believe it.'

THIRTY ONE

Oxford: October 1995

The two women had certainly 'been through the mill' since Rosalind's death. Barbara and Sean had taken on the main arrangements for the funeral, with help from Caroline and David, who were able to track down a great many people via the Faculty Office. They had discovered that Rosalind had only one living relative: a great-nephew of Henry's, named Clive Hawthorne, who was a vicar in Surrey. They had met him at the funeral and since then had spoken on the phone several times. These conversations grew increasingly difficult as the implications of there being no Will grew apparent.

As Rosalind's sole surviving relative, in the absence of a Will, Clive stood to inherit everything she had owned—including both houses in Oxford. He seemed amenable enough towards Mags and Barbara remaining in the houses short-term, but had said to David that eventually, he would probably sell the houses. David felt compelled to tell Mags and Barbara this, and did so after speaking with Sean. Everyone was left feeling insecure and worried.

The funeral itself had been the most emotionally draining that Barbara had ever witnessed. She had organised a few 'non-religious' funerals for relatives of friends in the past, and Mags was so relieved to have her there, knowing what to do. Mags chose to have Kirsty McColl's version of 'Days', the old Kinks classic, played as people arrived at the crematorium. 'It's my thanks to her,' she said to Barbara and Sean. 'The words are so right—'*And though you're gone, you're with me every single day, believe me.*'' They also included Sandy Denny's

'*Who Knows Where the Time Goes?*' as they remembered the effect the song had on Rosalind at the garden party.

Barbara helped Mags to write a very moving 'eulogy' which recognised Rosalind's academic achievements, her love of travel, and sense of fun. Even as they wrote it, they knew that neither of them would be able to read it at the funeral and were thankful to Sean, who stepped in and read it, adding a few words of his own in introduction.

Barbara had prepared a buffet for people coming back to the Lonsdale Road house afterwards, but was surprised that so many came; there must have been nearly a hundred people there. Even Gareth had been decent and nice to her when they met at the crematorium. At one point, to get away from the hubbub, Barbara stood in the hall, gazing out at the garden. Sean came and found her there. 'Are you all right, love?' he asked, slipping an arm around her shoulders.

'I guess so,' she replied with a sigh. 'Although I'm beginning to wonder if I'll ever be 'all right' again. I was just looking at the garden and thinking about the party . . . that night—do you remember? . . .' She broke off as tears came again.

'Aye, of course, of course,' Sean drew her to him and let her cry, her head against his chest. 'It was a special night, and we'll always remember it,' he said. Barbara lifted her head. 'Where's Mags?' she asked, stepping back from Sean and fishing a tissue from the supply in her jacket pocket.

'She's sitting quietly in the drawing room with Caroline. Do you know, I'm really surprised how well she's got through today? I feared for her—well, for both of you—that it would all be too much. I should have realised that you are both 'women of substance'!'

'I've a feeling that 'quality', if that's what it is, is going to be put to the test in the coming weeks and months.' Barbara said, gazing out once more on the garden.

It was now two weeks later. Mags stood in the kitchen at Lonsdale Road, an official-looking letter in her hand. 'I just don't understand it,' she said, flopping into a chair, handing the letter to Barbara, who scanned it quickly.

'How on earth can there be no record of Rosalind's Will?' she said. 'This just says that there is no Will lodged with these solicitors. Yet didn't you say that she always used this company? Could she have used another solicitor? We really need to know, soon, what this means for us, don't we?'

'I got in touch with them because it was a man from that company whom Rosalind said she'd met and told him what she intended to do, but it seems he died in May. He had been Henry's solicitor and was very old.

'But when was this meeting? Surely they have a record of an appointment or something?'

'No, she just asked him here for coffee one morning, before we went to Turkey. Then when we were there—it was that day we first met you—Rosalind showed me what she'd arranged, she had the document there, in Istanbul. She'd discussed it with her solicitor, she said, and was going to have it 'finalised' when we got back to Oxford. Just handwritten on a 'Last Will & Testament' pro-forma—like you'd buy at WH Smith—typically practical Rosalind. We were in the lounge at the hotel. I thought she'd taken it back to Oxford and done whatever one does with such things—given it to her solicitor. . . .'

'Well there IS a Will then!', Barbara slapped her hands on the kitchen table. 'It's got to be here in the house if she didn't give it to the solicitors. But why didn't she give it to them? It doesn't make sense.'

'It was only the day before Henry died—she had to go back to Oxford to sort everything out if you remember? Perhaps with all of that going on, she just forgot about it.'

'That doesn't sound like Rosalind, she wouldn't forget something so important, would she?'

'Oh Barbara, I don't know. I'm so frightened that I'm going to be separated—cut off, I mean, from everything to do with her. She was the most important person in my life. She had begun to be a little forgetful, in recent months, actually. But I just can't believe all this about the Will, it's bizarre. What will happen if we can't find it? I don't want to be over-dramatic, but I'm afraid and I feel time is running out. It could get to the stage when we are no longer allowed to go through her things—as we're not 'family'. That would be dreadful. We'll just have to search the house again. There's certainly nothing left in her room at college, David and Sean went back to check last week.'

'I don't think there's anywhere left to search,' said Barbara, standing up. 'But we could just go through the big desk again, and the box files, in the study, I suppose.'

Sean had stayed in Oxford, sleeping either on Barbara's sofa-bed in the lounge of her flat, or in the spare room at Lonsdale Road, since they arrived back from Ireland. He'd been able to extend the leave he'd already arranged at work for Barbara's visit, and had been a great help to the two women. Now he arrived at the back door with croissants and bread from the French patisserie in Summertown. As they ate them and drank coffee, they told him about the latest letter from the solicitors, and the increasing urgency to find the Will. Breakfast finished, they all went into Rosalind's study. Barbara and Mags sat on the floor, Sean sat in a chair by the bookshelves.

'If you and I take out everything in each of the pedestal drawers,' Barbara said, 'then lay it out on the top of the desk as tidily as we can, we can go through it methodically. Sean, will you tackle the box files up there?'

Sean agreed and the three of them set to work. It took a long time, for every few minutes something would be discovered that sparked a memory, and a story, from Mags—a postcard, a ticket, a photograph.

'By the way,' Sean looked across at Mags. 'This Clive, the nephew or whatever he is, was he at Henry's funeral?'

'Well if he was, I didn't notice,' Mags replied. 'And I wasn't introduced to him. He didn't say anything much to me at Rosalind's funeral, either. Why?'

'Just wondered,' Sean replied.

Barbara had stood up and was looking out of the window. 'Mags,' she said without turning. 'Tell me again what you said this morning, about Rosalind showing you the Will when you were in Istanbul.'

'Like I said, what we're looking for is just a handwritten form like you get from a newsagents', it's not even typed out, and . . .'

'No, not what it looks like, tell me what happened that day.' Barbara cut in sharply. Sean looked at her quizzically, surprised at her tone.

'Oh—we, er, well, we were in the hotel. She showed it to me and we talked. We met you then, didn't we? At the reception desk. Mehmet was there. Then later we went to that lovely café at the museum.'

Barbara didn't answer immediately. She was aware of the birdsong in the garden. She looked down at the postcard of Istanbul in her hand. Rosalind had sent it to Henry on their first day in the city. She tapped the card against her other hand as she turned to face Mags and Sean.

'I know where the Will is,' she said.

THIRTY TWO

Ataturk Airport, Istanbul, mid-October 1995

'*Merhaba*, Miss Barbara and Miss . . . Mrs, I mean . . .?' Osman blushed with embarrassment.

'Oh Osman it's so good to see you again!' Barbara kissed him on both cheeks. 'This is Mags, you remember?'

'Of course,' he replied, 'I am sorry, I do not know what is polite to say—to call you, I mean.'

Mags reached forward to shake hands: 'Just 'Mags' will do fine,' she said, smiling at Osman.

'Come, we must go to the car—Salih Bey is waiting outside,' he said as he picked up two of their bags and led them through to the exit.

As she had stood in Rosalind's study that day, looking out of the window, Barbara thought back, trawling her memories of the time she had met Rosalind and Mags at the hotel. It had seemed such a long time ago, but concentrating hard, she gradually remembered Mehmet tidying documents, keys and envelopes together and locking them in the hotel safe. She could clearly picture him doing so in her mind. That was when she realised that Rosalind had been giving him an envelope when she first spotted her with Mags at the Reception Desk at The Meydan.

When she explained this to Mags and Sean, they agreed that it had to be worth following up, and they phoned The Meydan that afternoon, managing to speak to Osman (didn't he ever go home?). He had said that there were certainly documents in the safe, but he would have to speak to the hotel's owner about removing anything, as "these are private things I am not allowed to touch"!'

Poor Osman, he feared that anything 'legal', especially anything to do with foreign hotel guests, would get him into trouble with his boss. He had the good sense to phone Mehmet, who had been very upset to learn of Rosalind's death, and who later called Barbara. During their long, emotional conversation, Mehmet confirmed that Rosalind had given him an envelope to put in the safe until she left, but that it had been completely forgotten by him, and seemingly by Rosalind, when it came to her unexpected departure following the news of Henry's death.

Later, Barbara couldn't really say how their 'plan' had come together so quickly, but by the time the phone call ended, Mehmet had suggested that he explain things to his uncle, Salih, who could speak to the hotel's owner, whom he knew, so that Osman would not have to worry about it. Barbara said she felt that she and Mags should go to Istanbul in person, to retrieve the Will, if indeed it was still there, even if it were just for a weekend. Mehmet called back the next day, by which time he had it all arranged—Salih was happy to help, and had even insisted on offering to let her and Mags stay in his flat above the bookshop if they were going back to Istanbul.

Sean had felt it unwise to contact the Oxford solicitors to ask them anything about this new development, because 'solicitors are in the business of thinking suspiciously', he'd said. So they had somewhat surreptitiously, via a solicitor friend of David and Caroline's, established that if a signed Will could be produced, and the signature verified as Rosalind's, it would be 'accepted' and legal. That done, they booked themselves onto a flight to Istanbul the following Friday evening. Sean went to Heathrow with them, as he was returning to Ireland at the same time.

So here they were, back in Istanbul. This time, on a mission.

Salih greeted them charmingly, bowing his head as he took in turn each woman's hand in both of his. 'Welcome, welcome. I am happy to greet you again,' he said, and held the doors open for them to climb into the back of the car.

'Salih, I must thank you so much for helping like this, it's very good of you.' Barbara said.

'I am honoured to be of help,' he replied as he swung the car around and headed for the city.

'I have arranged for us to meet Tariq Bey, the hotel owner, tomorrow, but not until the afternoon, at two. I have prepared a small meal for you tonight, and in the morning you can rest.'

As they drove along the ring road, past Kumkapi Gate, Barbara remembered the meal there with Mehmet on the first night of her last visit to the city. The night of the storm. The night of the floods. She looked at Mags who, without speaking, took her hand and squeezed it. So much had happened since then. Now, back in the streets where the 'first scenes' of their shared story had been played out, Barbara felt herself welling up; tears fell down her cheeks.

'I know,' said Mags, quietly, 'I know.'

They drew up in front of the courtyard leading to Salih's bookshop and Osman took their luggage from the boot.

'Here we are,' said Salih, as he opened a door at the side of the shop entrance. 'Welcome to my home, I hope you will be comfortable here.'

Osman carried the bags up the stairs and then took his leave, as he was 'Duty Manager' and had to stay at the hotel overnight. When he had gone, Salih showed Barbara and Mags to a large bedroom with two single beds. Behind a curtain was a small alcove with a dressing table and wash basin.

'If there is anything you need, please ask me,' said Salih. 'Now, when you are ready, please to come down and eat.'

Barbara sat on one of the beds. 'Well,' she said. 'It's so odd being back here isn't it?'

'Yes, more than odd, it's surreal,' Mags replied, 'But I'm so glad we've friends here to be with. It was great of Mehmet to ask Salih to help us. Osman, too, they're so good to us.'

They each had a quick wash, changed their clothes and went down to find Salih had laid out a delicious spread of *mezes* on a circular table in the kitchen-diner, with two places set.

'Are you not eating as well, Salih?' Barbara asked him.

'Oh no, I ate earlier, this is for you only.' He set down a bowl of pilau and returned to the kitchen. 'Would you like to have some wine, ladies?' he asked.

'That would be lovely, thank you,' Barbara replied.

'It will help you to sleep, I think,' Salih said as he reappeared at the table with a jug of red wine.

'And then we have an important day tomorrow, when I hope all will be arranged for you. I am so sorry to learn of your friend's death. It is right that these 'legal' things should go well for you now.'

'Thank you, Salih,' Mags was moved by his words. 'Thank you for your hospitality and for your kindness.'

'It is my pleasure,' he replied. 'Now, enjoy your meal, I will leave you. Please come through to the lounge when you have finished. I am going to watch the TV—the news.'

Barbara and Mags enjoyed the many little dishes that Salih had prepared for them. As they ate, they could hear the television from the next room, and now and then, Salih's voice: 'Aye, aye, aye,' in an exasperated tone. They cleared the table and washed the dishes, then carried their wine through to join Salih.

'Ah, ladies, have you eaten enough? Is there anything else I can do for you?' Barbara touched his shoulder, 'No, thank you, Salih, it was lovely. We heard you—were you commenting on the news? What is it you are watching?'

'Ah, it is the news from Afghanistan,' he replied, moving newspapers from the settee so that Mags and Barbara could sit down.

'My sister is in Kabul, her husband is from that place. I am very worried about what is happening there, I fear she is in danger, her and her young son.'

Barbara didn't know very much about what was going on in Afghanistan, but, it seemed, Mags did. She and Salih began to talk about recent events there and how Kabul was under siege, with frequent rocket attacks by the Taliban. Salih explained how he wanted to get his sister and her family out of the city and back to Turkey—to Anatolia where many members of his large family still lived.

As he said this, Barbara realised that his family was also Mehmet's family, Salih being his uncle. *'What a lot of worries for one family to cope with,'* she thought to herself as Salih and Mags continued to discuss the politics and history of the conflict.

'I do not know what to do,' he said, passing his hand over his eyes. 'I do not know if it is possible for her to leave. Perhaps I will go there and try to help her. It is a bad situation.'

Barbara suddenly felt very tired, so said 'goodnight' and went to their room, leaving Mags and Salih to their conversation. She was happy to see Mags bright-eyed and animated, as she used to be when they talked with Rosalind.

As she drifted into sleep, with the murmur of their voices drifting up from downstairs, she sent out thoughts, and love, to Mehmet and to Sean, knowing that each of them would be thinking about her and Mags, and wondering what would be the outcome of their 'mission' in Istanbul.

THIRTY THREE

Barbara and Mags sat on one of the large sofas in the front lounge of The Hotel Meydan. Barbara had a small notebook open on her lap; she fiddled nervously with a pen. She and Mags had been hit by a 'gale-force' sense of *deja-vu* when they had arrived with Salih, which had left them silent and thoughtful.

Salih had introduced them to Tariq Bey, the owner, who greeted them formally but kindly, and the two men were now speaking in Turkish while the women waited to be included in the proceedings. Yet again, Barbara thought their conversation was becoming heated, when Salih turned to them: 'Tariq Bey would like to know if you will take some *chai*,' he said, looking a little disconcerted when Barbara laughed out loud.

'Oh, forgive me, Salih, it's just that I thought you were saying something serious and important!' she said. 'Yes, tea would be good, thank you.'

Salih smiled. 'I think to you English ladies tea IS important, no?' And he spoke again to Tariq Bey, who called out to a young woman in the lobby to bring them tea.

The two men then resumed their conversation, leaving Barbara and Mags nothing to do but sit rather awkwardly, nodding and smiling whenever one of the men made eye contact.

When the tea arrived, there was a pause while they dealt with the tiny glasses and saucers, sugar lumps, spoons,—all the little 'doll's house'-type paraphernalia associated with it. Once they were all settled, Salih spoke again.

'Tariq Bey would like first of all to offer his condolences to you for the loss of your great friend,' he said. 'He hopes that our business here will be successful and that it will be comfort to you to have been among friends here in Istanbul who wish you well.'

Barbara and Mags nodded their thanks to Tariq Bey.

Salih continued: 'He respects my nephew, Mehmet, as he does all of my family, and says that he was a very good manager of the hotel. He knows that his words are to be trusted, and also that you esteemed ladies are of very good character. As the owner of the hotel, he has responsibility for the possessions of his guests—documents, money, passports and so on entrusted to him. So that he needs to be sure of the identity of anyone claiming any of these things from him. He is sure that you understand this, and he is glad that you have troubled yourselves to come here in person to see him.

Salih paused and exchanged glances with Tariq Bey, who nodded and reached for a document holder on the coffee table. 'Now, if you would like to look, he thinks these are the papers you are seeking, that belonged to your friend, Mrs Rosalind.' Salih took the large envelope from Tariq Bey and moved to give it to Barbara, who indicated with her hand that he should give it to Mags instead. Mags looked at Barbara, then at the envelope, as she took it, her hands were shaking.

'This is it,' she said in a whisper. I know it is, I remember.'

She lifted the unsealed flap and pulled out the contents. It was just as she had described to Barbara and Sean—a 'pro-forma' document, ready-printed with 'The Last Will and Testament of', and completed in Rosalind's distinctive handwriting. Mag's face creased in grief and she cried bitterly.

'There now, love, it's OK, it's OK,' Barbara put her arm around Mags and comforted her. 'Isn't this what we've been waiting for, so? Isn't this exactly what she would have wanted us to do?'

'Yes, oh yes,' Mags sobbed. 'It's just seeing her writing, and being here. To think that the last time I saw this I was with her and we were having such a lovely time.' She took a deep breath and looked at Salih. 'Please excuse me, I shall be all right in a moment.'

'There is no need,' Salih replied. 'Would you like to go to the bathroom, perhaps? We will wait for you and smoke while you are gone.'

Barbara really could have done with a cigarette herself, but went with Mags to the Ladies loo on the first floor, remembering how she had cleaned the staircase on the night of the floods, and been mistaken for a Turkish chambermaid! So many memories.

Freshened up, the two women returned to the lounge, where they noticed the pungent smell of Turkish cigarettes.

'Salih, would it be all right if I had a cigarette?' Barbara asked. 'I don't want to be impolite.'

'Of course, of course,' he replied, 'It is no problem,' and he started to offer her his own.

'No, thank you, I have some here in my bag,' she said. 'Yours are too strong for me!' This seemed to amuse Tariq Bey, who beamed at her.

'What do we do now?' Mags asked, of no-one in particular.

'Well, just please tell me that it's signed, for a start,' Barbara said.

Mags showed her Rosalind's signature and the date at the end of the document.

Barbara looked questioningly at Salih: 'Thank goodness for that. But yes, what *do* we do now, Salih?'

'Tariq Bey would like you to sign a book—is it a 'register' you say?—he has for these items from the safe, to show that he has given the document to you, and that is all.'

Salih turned and spoke to Tariq Bey, who from his briefcase produced a ruled exercise book which didn't look like it had been used until that moment. Barbara smiled at the trouble he had gone to—probably he had bought it only that morning in order that everything would appear professional and 'correct'.

Tariq Bey and Mags bent over the book and she signed it in several places he indicated. That done, he shook her hand feverishly, 'Thank you, Mrs, thank you,' he said. Relief of tension made them all laugh, and as they stood up, Salih suggested a drink in the bar to celebrate the 'good business' they had conducted.

On their way to the bar, Mags whispered to Barbara: 'I can't believe that's *it*, I thought there might be solicitors involved, or at least a policeman present!'

'I know what you mean,' Barbara replied, taking her arm. 'Turkish men always seem so serious and grave about what they call 'Business', but I guess this was just a case of whether he trusted us or not. It was all quite simple, really. I think it helped that Mehmet and Salih know him and vouched for us. What are you laughing at?'

'"Esteemed ladies" indeed!', Mags giggled.

'"Of very good character"!', Barbara replied. 'Now I'm going to shatter his illusions and have me a large brandy!'

Later, Barbara and Mags sat at the dining table in Salih's flat. He had opened the bookshop when they returned from the hotel and the two women had gone for a lie-down—brandy in the afternoon, combined with emotional exhaustion, having a soporific effect. It was now early evening, and they had just read through Rosalind's Will.

'So the old chap witnessed her signature, it seems,' Barbara said, pointing to the end of the document. 'That's why I find it odd that there was no record of it at the office in Oxford.'

Mags sighed. 'All I can think is that he was going to do all the 'official' stuff once Rosalind gave it back to him, which of course she never did. And then the poor man died.'

'Still, at least they can't quibble about the authenticity,' Barbara said.

'I do hope not,' said Mags. 'I can't help worrying that the solicitors will think it's suspicious, somehow. I keep feeling I've done something wrong.'

'Solicitors always make people feel like that, love. I'm sure you don't need to worry. Look at what David and Caroline's friend told us. But all we can do is take it back with us and go to see the solicitors next week—in fact, that particular office wouldn't have been involved at all if Clive Hawthorne hadn't started talking with them, assuming that no Will would be found and that they'd be acting for *him* in all this.'

'That's true,' Mags replied. 'He's not going to be very happy is he?'

'Actually, from what David told me, he sounds quite amenable. I think it was just that he thought it unlikely that the Will would be found. There's nothing left to him in the Will at all, is there?'

'No, but I feel rather embarrassed that it is all left to me. Of course, this was done before Henry died, so does that mean that all that Rosalind inherited from him is now part of her 'estate'?'

'I think it does, yes, but we'll have to check that out next week.'

'I feel even more embarrassed about it if that's the case,' said Mags, pulling a face.

'I can understand that, but you were the most important person in her life so it's not surprising, is it, that she provided for you in her Will?'

'It "provides" me with far more than I will ever need, the property alone is worth heaps.'

'Well, that's all to be thought about, but not now. I don't know about you, but I'd like to go out tonight and have a walk about, and maybe Salih would allow us to treat him to dinner—to thank him for what he's done.'

'Oh yes, let's!' said Mags. 'Could we go to . . . oh, but you may not want to . . .'

'Where?'

'I was wondering if you would mind if we went to that roof-top restaurant, next to The Meydan. But I don't mind if you would rather not.'

'Of course I don't mind,' Barbara said, taking Mag's hand. 'It would be a fitting place to go, I think, and we can drink a toast to Rosalind when we're there.'

'And to Mehmet,' Mags added.

'And to all our friends back home—Sean, David, Caroline—we're very lucky to have them. By the way, I was so happy to see you chatting away to Salih last night, you get on well with him don't you?'

'Yes, it was lovely to talk to a kind, intellectual man like him. He told me a lot about his life and his family. He may well go to Afghanistan to help his sister escape from Kabul, but it's very dangerous. He asked me to stay in touch with him, which I certainly will do. I do hope he'll be safe.'

'They all seem to have such "big" things to deal with,' said Barbara, looking from the window at the small fountain in the courtyard. 'I mean, look at what Mehmet's been through, then there's his brother for him to worry about, and now we learn that his aunt's holed-up in Kabul!'

'Well, for tonight, let's try to take Salih's mind off his troubles,' Mags said, rising from the table. 'I'll go down and ask him to join us later.'

THIRTY FOUR

There are moments, 'epiphanies' in time, that one remembers always; that evening was one of these for Barbara and for Mags.

Salih had said there was no need for such a gesture to thank him, that just to be able to help them was sufficient, but they managed to persuade him to join them by telling him how sad they would be if he did not.

The place was just as they remembered it; they recognised some of the waiters, who in turn realised who Barbara and Mags were.

'You are friend with Mehmet?' one of them said to Barbara as he greeted them and showed them to a table. 'You were here before?'

She nodded, and Salih quickly explained to him in Turkish that they were back in Istanbul having a short holiday with him.

'You are very welcome,' the waiter said as he bowed to them.

As before, they were looked after very well throughout the meal; the waiters' subtle attentiveness causing their presence to be almost unnoticed. The result was that the whole evening went smoothly and felt perfectly relaxed.

During the meal, Salih told Barbara and Mags more about his life; of how he came to open the bookshop after he had been the first in his family to go to college and to get formal qualifications. His achievements and recognition in calligraphy were an obvious pleasure to him, but he spoke of his worries about giving up both this interest and the bookshop itself if, as seemed to be the case, he was going to travel to Afghanistan in search of his sister and her family.

'I do not know if I will return to Istanbul,' he told them. 'If I am fortunate and bring my sister back to Anatolia, to the family, how long will it be to do this? My shop will be closed up and customers will forget it, and me. Perhaps there will be nothing to come back for. It will be like starting again from the beginning.'

'We are just so concerned that you are going to such a dangerous place,' Mags said. 'I can understand that you feel you must try to find your sister, but please be very careful if you do go.'

'Is there not anyone you know here who could run the shop for you, while you are away?' Barbara asked.

'Sometimes I have thought of this also,' he replied. 'But there is not much time to organise things, and people have their own business, their own work and families to care for. I wish that Mehmet was here, he would have liked to be in the shop, maybe. But he is not able to come back—he would have to go to the army.'

'That would have been a very good idea,' said Mags, 'What a shame that he can't do that, he would have enjoyed that, Barbara, wouldn't he?'

'I'm sure he would have, yes, but he's stuck for a couple of years, isn't he? And don't forget he has a son to think about now, as well.'

The three of them then spoke about Mehmet's situation, and the unhappy series of events he'd been through in the past year. Salih told them how Mehmet's mother, his sister, had been so proud of her son when he started at college, and how worried she now was about him, she relied on Salih for news, as it was difficult for Mehmet to contact her in the remote village where she lived.

'But the younger boy, Mehmet's brother, is now doing well,' Salih told them. 'I hope he will go to college here, he is sixteen now and wants to be an engineer.'

'Oh goodness, Ali, of course,' said Barbara. 'I forget that he must be growing up—not a schoolboy for much longer.'

'I was sorry that I could not help him more,' said Salih, lighting a cigarette. 'I gave Mehmet some small amounts of money sometimes, but I could not have Ali to live with me, he was in need of someone with time, to watch for him—do you understand?'

'You mean that he needed to be with a family—needed discipline and routine? Yes, Mehmet explained that to me,' said Barbara. 'I'm sure that it's been better for him to be with the family he's with. Mehmet said that he was happy and settled with them. Do you see him very often?'

'Oh yes, he comes to the shop some afternoons with his friends from school,' Salih replied. 'You have not met Ali?'

'No, I've only heard about him from Mehmet.' Barbara said.

'If you would like, we could meet him tomorrow perhaps? I am sure he would like to see you.'

'Does he know about me?' Barbara said, a little surprised. 'He knows that you are a dear friend of Mehmet's,' Salih said, smiling. 'And that is what you are, to our family, also. You care about Mehmet, and also about what happens to people. You are a very 'human' lady, I am knowing this, the same for you, Mags.'

'Sure, don't be making me out to be a saint!' Barbara laughed, embarrassed by Salih's words. But she said that she would certainly like to see Ali, so Salih agreed to make arrangements for them to meet the following day.

They walked back to the bookshop after their meal, still chatting about their memories of being there with Rosalind, and with Mehmet; they told Salih about places they had visited, and Mags reminisced about what Rosalind had thought and said about where they had been, people they had met. It was late when they returned to the flat, and Salih seemed tired, so they said goodnight to him and went to their room.

'What a lovely evening,' said Mags as she kicked off her shoes. 'Wasn't it nice to talk with Salih tonight? Although we don't 'know' him very well—haven't known him long, I mean—I really feel close to him now that he's shared so much with us.'

'Yes, I know what you mean, exactly,' Barbara replied. 'It seems odd that all this time there was another "element" to Mehmet's story—Salih, I mean. When I met him before, I didn't really think about his involvement—his feelings, and the family's worries about Mehmet. And now we're going to meet Ali. I feel a bit nervous about that, to be honest, and a little embarrassed.'

'Why? Because you and Mehmet were lovers, you mean?'

'Ha! That sounds like something out of a "bodice-ripper" novel!' Barbara laughed. 'But yes, I guess that's why. I'm sure that any sixteen-year-old boy is going to know what is meant by 'a dear friend' of his brother.'

'Well, Salih doesn't have a problem with it, obviously,' said Mags, picking up her dressing gown and going into the alcove room to wash. 'And I'm sure that he must know that you were 'more than friends', aren't you?'

'I imagine so. But that's just it—we *were* "more than friends", we were lovers, like you said. But then we weren't, and then so much happened to him, with Gul, the baby and everything. Then there's Sean . . . Yes, love, I am very fond of him but you know that we aren't 'lovers'. . .'

'Not yet,' Mags called from the alcove.

'You're probably right, so I shan't tell you off for making assumptions!' Barbara replied.

'But now we're back here, it all seems—oh, I don't know— 'backwards and forwards', somehow. I feel that since we've been here, I've been immersed in Mehmet's life again, having got used to 'detaching' myself from him over the last year.'

'How do feel about him, emotionally, when you think about him now,' Mags asked as she came back into the room and got into bed. 'Any different to when you were at home last week?'

'Not especially. I'm glad to learn more about his family, but I don't think of him with regret—as a 'lost love', if that's what you mean?' Barbara was now changing into her nightclothes in the alcove room.

'Hmm . . .' she heard Mags say. 'And Sean?'

'I'm just going to roll with it and see what's happens,' Barbara replied, getting into her bed. 'Go with the flow', as Rosalind would have said. Now let's stop mulling over my love life and go to sleep! Goodnight, love, *iyi geceler.*'

'*Iyi geceler, canim. Teşekker ederim herşey için.*' ('Goodnight dear. Thank you for everything'.)

'My! Your Turkish is coming on, isn't it?' Barbara looked at Mags in surprise.

'Well, Rosalind helped me when I was starting to learn the language, she was pretty fluent, you know? And I began to feel more confident speaking Turkish with Salih last night.'

'Good for you!' Barbara said, genuinely pleased for her friend. 'But you don't have anything to thank me for I've really enjoyed coming back here with you.'

'I didn't mean just this trip,' said Mags. 'I mean 'thank you' for being my friend, for helping me through the last few weeks especially. I want you to know that I really appreciate your friendship. But now I'm going to put out the light and go to sleep or I'll get all emotional again. Goodnight.'

'Goodnight love, sweet dreams of happier times ahead,' Barbara said, warmly.

She lay awake after Mags switched off the lamp, doing exactly what she'd told Mags they were to stop doing—mulling over her relationships—listening to Mags' quiet breathing as she slept, until she, too, fell asleep.

THIRTY FIVE

After breakfast the next morning, Salih told them he was going to drive over to the family Ali was staying with and ask if he wanted to come back into town with him. He suggested they meet at the café at the entrance to Gulhane Park at one o'clock, where they could have some lunch together.

Barbara smiled at the mention of the park, remembering the time that she and Mags had walked there, on another Sunday, when she had felt embarrassed at Mags' explicit description of her relationship with Rosalind in the hearing of so many people.

Once Salih had left, she and Mags went to their room and started to pack a few of their things in readiness for their departure next morning. That done, they walked over to the precincts of Sultan Ahmet and as they walked and chatted, continued across the road, where they paused opposite The Hotel Meydan. Just as they did so, Osman appeared from the front entrance, saw them, and waved as he trotted over to join them.

'Miss Barbara! Mrs . . . er, Mags!' he greeted them, beaming. 'How are you? Fine I hope? Where are you going?'

'We are just walking,' replied Barbara. 'We are meeting Salih later, and, we hope, Mehmet's brother, Ali, too—he's gone to get him now, if he wants to come.'

'Ah—Mehmet will be pleased that you meet his brother, I think,' Osman said. 'But would you like to come for coffee? I invite you,' he held his arm out towards the hotel.

Barbara and Mags exchanged glances before Barbara replied, 'Why not? Yes, thank you Osman,' and they went across to the hotel bar.

They sat at the bar with their coffee—cappuccino that Osman had so proudly made for them. The three of them chatted and laughed together, glad of the light-hearted 'banter' after so much gravity and 'serious business', as Tariq Bey would have called it.

Osman was in the middle of telling one of his stories about life at the hotel; he looked up at them enthusiastically, but as he did so, his expression changed and he stopped talking. His eyes darted from the window to Barbara and back again.

'Sorry . . . I must . . . I will come back . . . sorry! One moment please!' he mumbled, as hurriedly, he half-skipped past them to the door.

'What on earth is the matter?' Mags said, craning her neck after Osman.

'I think he saw someone coming past the window, into the hotel. Maybe just guests wanting their key.' Barbara said, draining her coffee cup. 'It's probably nothing.'

'But he looked worried to death,' said Mags.

Barbara was looking in her bag for her cigarettes when she heard Mags very obviously clear her throat. She glanced at Mags who tilted her head towards the door. Following her gaze, Barbara swivelled round and caught her breath as she saw Osman standing there with Gul's brother, Şerif. 'Şerif! Hello—how are you? I . . .' she stopped as Şerif strode over to her and placed his hands on her shoulders.

'Barbara,' he almost whispered her name. 'I am pleased to see you again, but so sorry to hear about your friend—the lady who has died.'

'Thank you, but I too must give you my condolences for—the terrible accident—for the loss of your sister. It was such a shock for your family, I am sure. How is your mother?'

'She is very much changed since the accident, all in my family are together in sadness,' he said, looking into Barbara's eyes as he spoke. 'But we *will* come through our troubles, *inşallah*.'

Osman was still hovering behind Şerif, looking at the floor.

Barbara looked away from Şerif and addressed him: 'Osman, come and finish your coffee—perhaps Şerif, you would like some too?' She indicated the bar stool next to her and Şerif sat down.

'And I must introduce Margaret Jenkins,' Barbara continued. 'My dear friend, who was Rosalind's companion for many years.'

Awkwardly, Şerif jumped to his feet again, and leaning across, shook Mags' hand, bowing his head. 'I am honoured to meet you,' he said solemnly.

Mags and Şerif began talking together, exchanging condolences and so on, as Osman made Şerif a strong, Turkish coffee, and placed it on the bar in front of him. Then he removed Barbara's empty coffee cup and slipped a small cup, without a saucer, in front of her on the counter.

'No, thank you, Osman,' she began to say, 'I don't want another . . .'

'Shh!' Osman pushed the cup towards her and winked. Barbara looked into the cup and saw that it contained not coffee but brandy. She smiled at him: 'Thank you,' she mouthed, and took a sip.

From his earlier awkwardness, and now this act of kindness, Barbara sensed that Osman was fully aware that she might feel uncomfortable with Şerif showing up unexpectedly. Could he know about what had happened in London? And if so, who had told him, Şerif himself, or Mehmet, during one of their phone conversations? Or maybe he thought it difficult only because of her relationship with Mehmet, and his with Şerif's sister. Whatever, Şerif and Mags were talking pleasantly enough, and after another sip of brandy, she felt calmer and turned back to join the conversation.

Şerif told them that he had gone to Baku after Gul's death and had brought her body back to Istanbul for her burial. After that, he had returned to Baku until only a week ago, to be with his brother's family and with Mehmet, as they organised for Ateş, the baby, to be cared for by his sister-in-law. Mehmet had been working very long hours at the casino; throwing himself into his job, Şerif thought, in reaction to the tragedy. 'He was saying, always, how he was guilty that Gul died,' Şerif explained. 'We all had to tell him this is not true; he was not to blame. He is better now, but he seems so tired. But he is with his son every day, he loves the child, I know.'

Barbara, caught Mags glance at her rather anxiously, she thought. 'Perhaps the baby is the one good thing to come out of it all,' she said. 'I know that you shared my fears for them both, getting into the situation they were in, not the best start to a relationship, marriage, whatever.'

'I agree with you, Barbara,' Şerif said, shaking his head slowly. 'It was not right for them to be together, he did not want that kind of life—to have a family.'

There was a short silence, broken only when Mags slipped down off her barstool, excusing herself to go to the Ladies. She reminded Barbara that time was getting on and they should be heading off to meet Salih at Gulhane Park.

Once she had left the bar, Şerif turned to Barbara, placing his hand on her arm.

'Barbara, about the time in London, I am sorry for . . . if I upset you.'

'It's OK, Şerif, I think we both had too much to drink, that day. It was just unfortunate that I was there on that particular day—when you got the news about the baby. Let's just put it behind us, shall we?'

'And we can be friends?'

'Of course we can—we *are* friends, Şerif.' And she leant forward to kiss his cheek.

Osman, who was witnessing all of this, busied himself polishing glasses and replenishing the coffee machine with water. When Mags returned, she and Barbara said their farewells and walked down the hill to Gulhane Park.

'Well, that was a bit of a surprise,' said Barbara. 'I suppose I should have realised that he could be in Istanbul again, I just didn't think about it at all.'

'I didn't know who it was, at first, but by Osman's behaviour, I thought it could be Şerif—that's why I coughed to warn you. Was it OK? He seemed to be talking very seriously to you when I came back from the loo.'

'Yes, it's fine. He was actually apologising for what happened when he came to London. Jesus, that seems so long ago and so unimportant now. Still, it was decent of him.'

'Rosalind used to say that most people are decent, given the chance,' said Mags, taking Barbara's arm. 'And as in so many things, I think she was right.'

THIRTY SIX

As they approached the café, they could see Salih standing, talking with a waiter; he seemed to be alone.

'Oh, that's a shame, he's on his own,' Mags said.

'Well, I guess sixteen-year-olds have better things to do on a Sunday than to come and meet a couple of English women!' Barbara replied, smiling. 'Although I must admit, I was curious to meet Ali.'

'But we are "esteemed ladies", don't forget,' laughed Mags. 'And I'm sure that Salih would have told him that!'

'That's probably why the poor lad didn't come!'

Salih saw them and raised his hand in greeting. '*Merhaba*—here you are!' he said, taking each woman's hand in turn.

The waiter leapt into action, pulling out chairs for Barbara and Mags, smoothing the tablecloth, flicking their chairs with his glass-cloth before they took their seats.

'This is nice,' Barbara said as she noticed there was already a selection of *mezes* and a carafe of white wine on the table. 'But there are four places set—I thought you were alone?'

'No, no,' Salih replied, pouring wine for them, 'Ali has gone to . . . there is something he wanted to do, he will be back soon.'

'I'm . . . we are so pleased he wanted to come,' said Barbara. 'We wouldn't have been surprised if he hadn't, most boys that age are wrapped up in their own friends and the places they go.'

'Ah, Ali is not like most young people,' Salih replied. 'He is very respectful of his family—and of anything connected with his elder brother. This is why he wants to come today. I think, also, he is wondering what you are like, Barbara. And, of course he has me, his uncle, inviting him for a pleasant lunch, which is another temptation!'

Barbara looked up as she sipped her wine; what she saw made her gasp and almost choke. 'That must be him, there,' she spluttered.

Mags followed her gaze and saw a younger, slighter, version of Mehmet coming towards them, carrying flowers.

'Why—he's just like Mehmet!' she said to Barbara, as Salih rose to greet Ali. Barbara looked dumb-struck.

Salih introduced them to Ali, who bowed his head as he presented each of them with a bouquet of flowers.

'I am sorry I am not here when you arrive,' he said. 'I must go for flowers to greet you.'

(Barbara heard her 'practical gremlin' on her shoulder, saying they wouldn't be able to take flowers home on the plane next day, but told it to 'shut up!'). Luckily, Mags had jumped in, thanking him warmly, before Barbara could find words; even his voice was like Mehmet's.

'Sorry, yes, thank you so much,' she managed to say at last. She glanced at Salih, who was smiling and nodding at her. 'I'm sure you must be told this all the time,' she said to Ali. 'But you are SO like your brother, it's incredible!'

'Yes, I know this. Many people tell me. But he is not ugly so this is OK, I think.' Ali said this without smiling—it was a serious consideration on his part. Nevertheless, the others all laughed and told him he was right, which did make him smile.

Throughout their lunch, Barbara was very aware that she was watching Ali, noting his every mannerism and turn of phrase. She was sure that Mags had noticed; she only hoped that the poor lad didn't feel uncomfortable if he'd seen her watching him, although he seemed fine as he chatted happily to everyone. By the end of their lunch, though, it was Barbara who began to feel uncomfortable: several times, Ali came out with comments about Mehmet and his relationship with Barbara. He obviously believed that she was in love with his brother, and seemed to think that now poor Gul was dead, there was nothing 'in the way' of Barbara becoming his sister-in-law! Salih was obviously embarrassed for Barbara, and laughed loudly at the first few of these, patting Ali's hand and trying to change the subject. But finally he spoke to Ali quickly, in a low voice in Turkish. He then pushed back his chair, as if preparing to leave.

'Mags, would you like to take a walk with me?' he said as he rose and moved next to Mags' chair, offering her his arm.

'Well, er . . . if you don't mind us leaving you two for a while?' she asked Barbara with a meaningful look. Barbara felt rather flustered, but said she'd be fine, and she watched the two of them move off, arm in arm, pausing to speak with the waiter who had taken their order. She reached across the table for a cigarette.

'Here, I will light,' Ali said, pouncing on her lighter.

'Thank you. Would you like one? I don't know if you smoke?' Barbara offered him the packet.

'Yes, please. I do not smoke in front of my uncle, or with the family—where I live, you know? But I do like to smoke sometimes. I know it is bad.' He took a cigarette and lit it; leaning forward, he pushed the end of it around in the ashtray in little movements, exactly as Mehmet had a habit of doing.

'Ali, the things you said earlier, I think I should . . .' Barbara began.

'It is OK, my uncle has told me I was not polite. I am sorry,' he said, looking directly at her, before lowering his eyes.

'I am so happy that Mehmet . . . when he meets you, you know? He told me he writes to you and then you come here. But then he is not happy and when he goes to Baku I am worried. I know that he loves you, Barbara. Then there is baby and everything, the accident—it is all bad for my brother, I think. I want him to be here, in Istanbul, but that cannot happen. I miss him. I want him to have a good life.'

He stopped and took a deep breath, exhaling in a long sigh. Barbara was moved to see there were tears in his eyes.

'Ali, love, I know it's been awful for Mehmet. And it's been hard for you—well, for all his family and friends—I know I felt that I wanted to help him but couldn't. If I could have waved a wand and put time back, so that none of it happened, I would have done, believe me. But what happened, happened, and we just have to get on with our lives from now on, with things the way they are.'

'But you love Mehmet, now?' Ali asked, looking intently at her again.

'As a friend, Ali. I can't say any more than that. Many things have happened, not just to Mehmet. I have had changes in my life in Oxford, too, you know? And some great sadness—my friend Rosalind died.'

'Yes, I am very sorry—my uncle tells me she was a very good lady, very good friend to you and to Miss Mags,' he drew on his cigarette before stubbing it out.

'Do you have a boyfriend in Oxford, at home, now?'

'Not exactly, but there is someone who has become special. He helped me and Mags when Rosalind died, and I would like to . . . well, to have a relationship with him, if it happens. He doesn't live in Oxford, though, so I don't know when I'll see him again.'

'So you will not be with Mehmet in the future?'

'Oh Ali, I don't know. At the moment it doesn't seem likely. Mehmet has to stay out of the country for quite a while, still, or he'll be carted off to the army. And he has his son to think about too. From what I've heard, he loves him, which I'm happy to hear. All I know is that we will always be friends. I'm sorry if you wanted to hear more from me.'

'No, it is my fault, wanting these things. I do not think about you—what you want. I am sorry. I hope that we can also be friends,' he replied, smiling.

'I hope so too, if you're not too disappointed that I'm not about to become your sister-in-law!' Barbara smiled at him cheekily, and he laughed, visibly more relaxed than when the conversation had started.

'Would you like more coffee?' he asked, glancing at their waiter who was passing the table.

Barbara said that she would, and while Ali spoke to the waiter, she turned to look across the park, at all the people walking, chatting, sitting on the grass. She spotted Salih and Mags, who were sitting on a bench under a huge tree, deep in conversation. She was so pleased to see Mags like this again; like she had been when talking with Rosalind. *'Obviously a meeting of minds,'* she thought to herself, *'and we all of us deserve to have that happen once in a while.'*

THIRTY SEVEN

Oxford, November 1995

A few days after their return from Istanbul, Mags had gone with David and Caroline to meet Henry's nephew, Clive Hawthorne, at the solicitor's office. They returned jubilant. Everything was 'above board', so far as the legality of Rosalind's Will was concerned, and Clive was very gracious in his acceptance of it. Mags had told him that she wanted to make him a small gift of money, once everything was sorted out, for which he thanked her, saying that he would donate it to a children's charity based in his parish.

Barbara had spoken to Sean several times, telling him the good news, firstly in retrieving the Will, and then the successful outcome of Mags' meeting. Barbara longed to see him again, but after all the time they had taken off work in the last few months, neither had any leave left to take until Christmas, but Sean had invited her to stay with him then. She told him all about the trip to Istanbul: even about Ali and his assumptions about her relationship with Mehmet. Sean was pleased to hear Barbara say that since their return, Mags seemed to have found a new strength. She had been cheerful, certainly in control, and was organising everything that needed to be done very efficiently. There was no sign of the timid, mouse-like woman whom Sean had worried would not be able to cope after Rosalind's death.

Three weeks later, on a Saturday morning, Mags was sitting in Barbara's kitchen, cupping a mug of coffee in her hands as Barbara removed a fruit cake from the oven, placing it on a chopping board to cool. Even for November, it was bitterly cold outside, and had been for several days.

'David and Caroline's friend, the solicitor, is going to go through all the financial stuff, such as tax and things for me,' she said to Barbara. 'It shouldn't take too long, he said on the phone. And then, my dear, I want to put my plans into action.'

'Oh yes?' Barbara replied, pouring herself a mug of coffee from the cafétiere. 'Are you going to tell me about them?'

'Well, you know that I want you to have this place, I've told you that already. But let's go into the sitting room—I want to run some things by you.'

So they took their coffee through to the other room. Seated on the sofa next to one another, Mags took Barbara's hand and continued:

'And please don't start objecting to what I'm going to suggest before you've heard me out,' she said, smiling.

'First of all, I would like you to have this house, not just the flat. I think it would . . .'

'But you can't just . . .' Barbara interrupted.

'What did I just say about not objecting? Treat this as a story I'm telling you, if you like. A 'what if' scenario, and let me know what you think at the END, all right? Now, no more interruption, please.'

Mags then outlined her 'plan', as she called it, to which she had obviously given much thought over the previous few weeks. She wanted Barbara to have the entire house in Staverton Road, so that she could have an income from renting out the top flat, as well as the security of her own property. Mags knew, she said, that Barbara had been growing unsettled at work, and this way, at least she would have the option of resigning, should she choose to, and to investigate freelance work, or to pursue 'other things'. Barbara was astonished, but let Mags continue. What she told her next astonished her even more.

'You know that Salih and I had many long conversations when we were in Istanbul, mainly about his wish to go to Kabul. I must admit that I shall be very worried about him, but he is determined to go and find his sister. He was worried about the shop—you know he spoke to us about shutting it up? Well, I asked him if there was any way of buying out Mehmet from having to do his National Service—you know, one hears about servicemen here buying themselves out of the term they've signed up for? But Salih explained that Mehmet would have to do that anyway, after three years out of the country—it seems that he could then return, pay a sum of money and serve for just one month in the army. So there doesn't appear to be any way of Mehmet returning to take on the shop as yet.'

Mags paused, drank the last mouthful of her coffee, and continued: 'So I have suggested to Salih that I go out to Istanbul to run the shop until such time as he returns, or we are able to get Mehmet back to take it over.'

'What? On your own?' Barbara gasped.

'Yes, it will be a good opportunity for me to improve my Turkish and to get on with some work I am doing on Afghanistan,' she said. 'But I hope that you will come out, often, to stay with me?'

'Jesus! Are you sure about this, Mags? I mean . . . it's a bit of a shock, that's all! What about Mehmet, has Salih spoken to him about all this?'

'Probably, by now. He was going to phone Mehmet last night. He is going to phone me at home tonight to tell me what happened. But Barbara, what do you think? I know it's a shock for you, but I really don't think it is a 'hare-brained' idea at all. I've thought about it very carefully and made sure of what is and isn't possible. Eventually, I might buy somewhere of my own in Turkey, but I don't need to think about that just yet. The thing is, I never dreamed of having so much— of being suddenly so wealthy, and I want do some good—to share my good fortune with others, so I'm looking into Trust Funds and setting up bursaries and so on, as well as these few things I can do to help you and our friends.'

'It's one hell of a lot more than a few things, love,' Barbara said, her eyes blurring, overtaken by a rush of emotion. 'It's all a bit much to take in. I'm just so grateful for our friendship, what we've been through together . . . and now all this . . .' she broke off with a sob.

'Come on, dear, it's all going to be fine,' Mags said, rubbing her hand on Barbara's back. 'If it wasn't for you, none of this would have happened, would it? We might have both been homeless; the houses would have been sold and everything would have gone to mend Clive's church roof or something!'

Barbara laughed despite her tears, 'And we know what Rosalind would have thought of that!' she said, taking Mags' hand in hers. 'Listen, it seems to me that you've taken this all on by yourself— figured it out, I mean, what to do, and how to do it. So the most gracious thing I can do is to accept my part in your plans, and I hope I can help you with some of those other things you want to do.'

'Thank you, dear. I was rather counting on your help. It's a big leap into the unknown, this 'starting a new life', isn't it?'

'What will you do with Lonsdale Road? While you are away, I mean?'

'It's a strange coincidence, but David and Caroline's daughter is returning to Oxford from Australia with her husband and their two young children. The husband's taking up a lecturing post at St Anthony's next year. Caroline was talking about trying to find a house for them to rent, so I suggested . . .'

'Young kids? Running about in your house? Surely that wouldn't . . .' Barbara blurted out.

'Oh, great minds!' Mags said, laughing. 'No, I realise that it's not exactly "child-friendly", so what I suggested was that if Caroline and David would like to move into my house, their daughter and her family could live in theirs, at least for a while, until they're settled back here. And I've insisted that they are doing me a favour in looking after the house and so they are to pay no rent. It's my way of thanking them for all their help and advice.'

'Oh Mags, that's great! I can't believe all this can really happen, but your excitement about it is contagious, I'm so looking forward to whatever comes next. It's all been a bit of an adventure hasn't it? Now, I could do with some fresh air, how about we wrap up and go for a walk on Port Meadow? We can take some apples for the horses.'

So they walked down to the Meadow, the grass crunching underfoot where it was still frosted in the shadows. When they reached the river, they turned and stood arm-in-arm, looking at the wintery Oxford skyline they loved so much, saying nothing, until shaken from their thoughts by a large bay horse announcing his presence with a loud snort.

THIRTY EIGHT

Donegal, Ireland, December 1995

The low afternoon sun slanted in through the window of Sean's cottage kitchen, illuminating fine clouds of flour dust around Barbara, who was busy making pastry. Now and then, she would pause, listening to the sounds drifting up from the cosy sitting room, where Sean was playing guitar and singing snatches of folk songs.

'That was nice, love,' she said over her shoulder as he entered the kitchen. 'My own kitchen concert, thank you!'

He stood behind her, his hands on her hips, and bent to kiss the back of her neck.

'Ach, the least I can do for the chef!' he said. 'What's the recipe today then?'

'I'm just doing some mince pies with that home-made mincemeat that your neighbour gave us yesterday—Mrs Patsy, is it? The one with all the chickens in the front of her cottage.'

'Aye, that's her. She's Mrs O'Dowd, really, but her husband was called 'Patsy', so we've always called her 'Mrs Patsy'. Sean sat on one of the stools next to the table where Barbara was working. 'Shall we give the chef a break and go down to the pub to eat tonight?' he asked.

'That would be good, but I'd like to get an early night, what with Mags arriving tomorrow,' she said. 'So if there's a session going on, we'll have to drag ourselves away and not get involved like the other night—Jesus, we didn't leave until gone two, did we?' she laughed.

Barbara had been there a week, and as she had hoped, their

relationship had been 'established' from the first day. When Sean met her at the airport they had kissed passionately and on arrival at his cottage they had gone straight to Sean's bedroom and made love, half-undressed, on top of the bed. Urgent and passionate though it was, it seemed so natural to them, without any 'first time' awkwardness or embarrassment. Later, they had laughed and talked all evening, preparing and enjoying their meal together; curling up on a deep, 'plumpy' sofa in front of the fire afterwards, with coffee and brandy. Barbara felt perfectly happy. Woven through her contentment were threads of excitement, in anticipation of the future, now that so much had changed.

She had talked with Mags several times more about the gift of the house as she had still felt uncomfortable about accepting such generosity. As Mags had reassured and encouraged her, she reminded Barbara so much of Rosalind—she spoke of 'practicalities' and 'the obvious and sensible course of action'. Barbara had also spoken about it all on the phone to Sean, who had said pretty much the same as Mags; given her the same reasons why she should accept her good fortune. With their help, Barbara had been able to put her qualms aside, and began coming to terms with her new circumstances. Of course, there was legal paperwork, and stuff to do with tax to be sorted out, to make it all 'official', but that, Mags said, could be tied up by the end of the year. So in the middle of November, she had given a month's notice to her astonished manager; organised her 'leaving bash' at a local Italian restaurant; and arranged to fly out to stay with Sean for Christmas.

Meanwhile, at the start of December, Mags had gone to Istanbul, to stay with Salih and make arrangements for when he left the shop in her hands. He hoped to leave for Kabul in the spring; travel during the Afghan winter being nigh-on impossible. Sean had suggested that Mags join them in the cottage for Christmas, and she had leapt at the idea. She was to arrive on the 21st December—the Winter Solstice. Barbara pointed out the significance of the date to Sean: 'A special time for a special friend to arrive,' she said, 'and for us to be together in a special place.'

'Will you just look at her,' Sean nodded towards Mags, coming through the Arrivals gate. 'She looks so different to when I last saw her.'

'I know, it's like I told you. I always thought of her as a timid little woman, but she's really not. If you think about it, she's done a lot of travelling, in her line of work, and she and Rosalind went to some pretty remote and unusual places, didn't they? So I guess she's pretty confident about travelling and getting around.'

'It's not just that though, it's the way she's handled everything after Rosalind . . . well, y'know. She's far more capable than I ever thought she was. But come on, she's coming out through there, look.'

Sean called out: 'Mags!', waving as they rushed across the concourse. Seeing them, she put down her bag and opened her arms to receive their hugs and kisses.

'Oh goodness, what a welcome!' she said. 'How lovely to see you both.'

'We've been here ages,' said Barbara, as Sean picked up the bags and they started to walk towards the exit. 'But the flight wasn't delayed, was it? It said on the screen that it landed on time.'

'Oh I know, it was dreadful, getting through once we'd landed. Everyone had to have their passports checked and they opened most of the bags. Now I know how it feels for people who have to join the 'non-UK passports' queues! I suppose anyone coming into Belfast from such a strange and exotic place as Istanbul is bound to be suspicious!' She gave them a wry look. 'But I'm here safely now, and longing for a cup of tea!'

'Well, we can fix that one for you on the way,' said Sean. 'There's a wee tea-room I know—we'll stop there.'

In the car, Barbara fired dozens of questions at Mags about her trip to see Salih; she wanted to know everything that had happened, she said, and all about their plans. Had she seen Osman? Şerif? How were they? 'Stop, stop! I'll tell you all about it but not now, dear!' Mags said, holding up her hands in front of her. 'We've plenty of time for talking while I'm here.'

Sean glanced in the rear-view mirror, smiling at Mags. 'And for lots of wining, dining, music and merriment, too!' he said, as he turned the car into the driveway of a pretty farmhouse, 'here we go now, this is the place for your tea.'

It was also, as they discovered, the place for very good cakes. As they enjoyed their tea, Mags satisfied Barbara's hunger for news of their friends, telling her that everyone was fine and had sent their greetings and love to Barbara. Mags then switched roles and became the one to ask questions of Barbara: 'So tell me about your last day at the office, how did it go?' she asked. 'And what do you think you'll do next? Have you thought any more about freelance work?'

'Hey! Now who's got too many questions, all at once?' Barbara laughed. 'But since you ask, I have been thinking about it. What I'd like to do is take some time off and see if I can get into travel writing, for guidebooks, magazines, y'know? Maybe even write a novel—I've got enough material in my addled brain, I'm sure!'

'That sounds like a good idea, you can always write, wherever you happen to be, can't you?'

Barbara agreed, and continued: 'It was kind of strange, though, those last few days at work. People would hear that I was leaving and come rushing up to my desk, full of questions—where was I going? Had I got another job? And so on. It was quite awkward, sometimes. Then all the usual meetings and briefings going on, but it seemed pointless my attending them, as I wasn't going to be involved in any of it. Still, it meant that I was glad when that last month was over. I'll always support the organisation's work—I've seen what a dramatic difference it can make to people's lives—but I'd had enough of the 'office politics' and the constant restructuring, I'm afraid. So thank you, Mags, for being my escape route!'

'My pleasure, my dear,' said Mags, brushing cake crumbs from her fingers onto her plate. 'I think you are already looking more relaxed than when you were working. I'm sure you'll make a go of whatever you decide to do.' She placed her napkin on her empty plate and turned to Sean.

'Sean, that was delicious and probably about eight hundred calories!

Please don't let me stuff myself silly while I'm here, because I can and will, most happily, if no-one stops me!'

'Well, we're having a 'Mrs Patsy' chicken for dinner tonight,' he said, laughing at Mags' puzzled face. 'And with Barbara's cooking, I think you should expect to gain a few pounds this week! I think it's allowed—sure, it's Christmas!'

THIRTY NINE

Mags loved Sean's cottage. It was twilight when they arrived, and Barbara had taken her along to her room while Sean stirred life back into the log fire in the sitting room. Mags wanted to unpack and take a bath, so Barbara left her to it while she started preparing their dinner. There were traditional Christmas tunes and songs on the radio, which she sang and hummed along to while she worked. Sean came in from the barn with a basket of logs for the fire and laughing, they harmonised a chorus together. The chicken in the oven, and vegetables prepared, Barbara poured herself, Sean and Mags a glass of Amontillado sherry, took Sean's to him in the sitting room, and on her way to the bedroom to change, she tapped on the bathroom door. Mags opened it wearing a light, satin bathrobe Barbara recognised as the one she had given to her the previous Christmas, from Azerbaijan. She'd given one to Rosalind as well. She smiled at the memory as she handed Mags the sherry.

'Ooh, drinking sherry in the bath—how decadent!' Mags said. 'I could get used to this, you know!'

'Well, why not? I'm just going to take a shower and tidy myself up a bit—no, I don't need to use the bathroom, there's a wee en-suite in our . . . er . . . Sean's room.' She felt herself blushing, but they both laughed. 'So take your time. The chicken's in, and before dinner we'll have plenty of time for a drink or two in front of the fire that Sean's 'creating' for us!'

Mags raised her glass to Barbara. 'Here's to us,' she said. 'And to our plans, may they bring happiness to many.'

'That's a nice toast,' said Barbara, chinking her glass against Mags'. 'Happiness to many, I'll drink to that.'

At the far end of the sitting room, Sean and Barbara had laid the dining table simply but beautifully, with small candles arranged with holly as a centrepiece. The glasses and cutlery shone, and the aroma from the kitchen made their mouths water as they had their drinks.

'This reminds me of an advert on TV when I was small,' Barbara said. 'Do you remember it? It was only on at Christmas, for cream sherry. There would be this lovely fireplace with a happy family around it, and friends arriving to stay, and then they'd all go off for a walk with dogs and kids. I remember my ma would always see it and say she wished she had nice dogs like that to go tramping off with across the fields! Although I remember thinking how unreal the advert seemed to me—having friends to stay, huge log fires, my Christmases were nothing like that!'

'Well, sure I'll try and make them more like that for you now,' Sean said, smiling at Barbara. 'If that's what you'd like? At least the friends to stay and the log fires. Haven't a dog though—not at the moment!'

'It would be nice to have dogs to walk in a place like this,' Mags said slowly and distractedly, looking into the fire. Barbara squealed with laughter.

'Mags, stop it—you're playing the part of my ma now!'

'Well it *would*,' Mags laughed. Talking about the advert started them off, and they reminisced over other old adverts, TV and radio programmes until it was ready to eat.

'I must say it looks fabulously festive, in a pagan way in here, you two,' Mags said as they sat around the table after dinner.

'That's what Barbara was up to before you arrived. I've never bothered much with decorations, but I love all the greenery and the candles,' said Sean.

Barbara gazed around the room. 'I've always found all the pagan festivals—the history and traditions surrounding them—far more interesting than the Christian ones,' she said. 'It feels absolutely right to celebrate Yule, in the dark days of winter. I love all the candles and food and cosiness! So even though I'm a 'devout atheist', I love this time of year!'

'So many of my friends feel like that, you know? I suppose it's not surprising, as most are anthropologists!' Mags said. 'How about you, Sean? You told me once that you were raised a Catholic but became atheist at Oxford—but is it difficult for you now, living in a small Irish community?'

'Not really,' answered Sean. 'The saving grace is that in the Gaeltacht areas, the people I work with and see most of are more interested in culture and history than in religion, on the whole. Sure, if you were to go to wee villages in the south, and announced yourself as an atheist, well, you just wouldn't do that.'

Barbara watched them talking, her wine glass cupped in both hands. She had always wanted evenings, meals, to be like this, with intelligent conversation laced with laughter and kindness. She put her glass down and joined in herself.

'Hmm, it's like when some of us from the Oxford folk sessions used to go carol singing in a few villages; some people couldn't understand me doing that, being an atheist, but it gave people such pleasure, especially the elderly ones, to hear the old tunes. That was my reason for doing it—it didn't matter to me if we were singing carols, nursery rhymes, or sea shanties!'

'Absolutely!' said Mags. 'I do so wish that we could see ourselves simply as human beings, without any of the divisive labels, religious or otherwise, we poor hairless apes are so keen to apply to ourselves. I'm sure the world would be a far kinder, happier place were it so.'

'Hear, hear,' said Sean, raising his glass to Mags. 'But it'll not happen in our lifetime, sadly. Now, shall we move to the fireside? I'll fetch another bottle, shall I?' and he went to the kitchen, where they could hear him clearing things away, humming In the Bleak Mid Winter to himself.

Barbara and Mags exchanged glances and smiled. They took their glasses and sat on the sofa. When Sean returned, they were talking about Mehmet.

'Yes, you know he phoned me after Şerif had spoken to him,' Barbara was saying. 'He was so happy, he said, to think of being able to run the shop one day, and to live there with Ali. He said a lovely thing—that he trusted the future would be positive because it was Rosalind's influence, and she was a very good woman.'

'Oh that *is* lovely, said Mags, her hand going to her face. I think he's right, her legacy isn't just about property and capital, is it? It's as Mehmet says: her influence, her spirit, which I'd like to carry on as best I can.'

'I had a letter from him, too,' Barbara said. 'It was so positive. He said that when he returns to Istanbul, Ali will live with him at the flat. He'll be at college by then . . .'

'Hey, Mags, they'll be evicting you, so you'll have to find somewhere else by then, or come home!' laughed Sean. 'Or you know you can always stay here for as long as you need, whenever you need.' He added, kindly.

'Thank you, dear. I'm so lucky to have so many 'homes', aren't I?' Barbara continued: 'Mehmet said that he will bring the baby back with him—well, he won't be a baby then, will he? He'll be a toddler. But anyway, he will live with Gul's mother in the Fatih area, not far from Beyazit, and Mehmet will see him often as he's growing up. But what about Salih's plans, how is he going to set about finding his sister? I've heard that thousands left Kabul in October, when the fighting was so bad. Obviously she didn't get out then or he'd know, or would he?'

'Not necessarily. People have disappeared—into the mountains, into Pakistan; communications are unreliable at best, and now the winter has set in—it's impossible to know. That's why Salih believes the only way to find out anything certain is to go out there himself. Poor man is so worried about what might have happened. Still, there's one development—there is a cousin, it seems, from Anatolia, who is willing to go with him, so at least he won't be alone. They will go to Pakistan first. After that, they'll have to play it by ear, depending on the situation. But who knows what will be happening there by March?'

While Mags had been speaking, Sean had poured them more wine and was now standing by the CD player. He looked up when Mags finished speaking.

'He's a brave man. All we can do is hope that it calms down out there and doesn't get any worse. It's always civilians who suffer most in war. It could be seen as an incongruous term, 'civil war', couldn't it? What the hell is 'civil' about it? OK, so it affects 'civil society'—but that's such an impersonal term, it doesn't bring to mind the women and children—the families who bear the brunt of it all.' He turned and put a CD on the player. A haunting, 'slow aire', played on a low whistle, filled the room. Sean sat on the floor, leaning back against the sofa, where Barbara and Mags had curled up at either end. All three were silent as they gazed into the fire, allowing the music to take them over. As the track came to an end, Sean drained his glass and spoke, still looking into the flames: 'Aye, but as you say, Mags, who knows what will be happening by then?'

Mags sighed. 'If there's one thing I think we've all learned in the last year,' she said drowsily, 'It's that our lives change when we're least expecting it. But if we're lucky enough to have dear friends to help us through the hard times, and with whom to share the good ones, we'll come through stronger for it in the end.'

FORTY

March 1996

Barbara had been back to Oxford for only two weeks since Christmas. She loved being with Sean and the two of them had fallen easily into a happy routine together. When Sean returned to work after the holidays, Barbara amused herself by walking out along the coast, capturing photos of the wild landscape. Or she would spend whole afternoons in the kitchen, baking and preparing delicious meals. Often, she would go to The Gaeltacht Centre, where Sean's work was based, to wander through the exhibitions, and to help out, too, with everything from picture research to working in the kitchen of the visitors' café. Before they knew it, Barbara had been in Ireland for nearly six weeks.

One blustery Sunday evening, as they talked after dinner about how the time had flown, Sean had asked Barbara if she would like to stay for 'a good while longer'. Barbara had replied that she couldn't see any reason why she would even *think* of disrupting the lovely time they were having. 'But I should go back for a bit,' she added, 'even if it's just to pick up some more clothes—I've only winter things with me.'

'You're forgetting this is Ireland, don't be expecting the spring until . . . ooh, at least July!' he laughed.

'Seriously, though, I'll go back and have a sort out. Caroline is going in to pick up the post but I have to admit, I don't like the thought of the flat being left empty, all this time. And now for longer, even.'

'You could let it out,' Sean suggested 'Like the top flat. Even short-term lets—you're bound to find tenants in Oxford!'

'Hmm, not sure about that. But I could ask Caroline, I guess; and people I used to work with—sometimes they need places for staff from overseas who are visiting. Actually, I'd be willing to do that for them for free. Just as long as they pay the electricity and phone bills, y'know?'

By the time Barbara arrived in Oxford, she had phoned her old work mates and had been delighted to find that Samira, her former colleague from Baku, needed somewhere to stay while on secondment to the Oxford office for six months. Barbara spent her first week in Oxford preparing the flat for Samira's arrival, cleaning and packing things away. She then met her friend at Heathrow and spent a few days with her, introducing her to other former colleagues and friends, meeting up with them in pubs and at music sessions. Barbara was relieved and happy that someone she knew and trusted would be living there while she was in Ireland with Sean. She liked her flat, and especially the garden, which Samira promised to look after, thrilled to have a garden after living in a fourth-storey city apartment since she was a child.

Meanwhile, Mags had been living at the bookshop since February. She had enrolled on a Turkish language course, and from her phone calls and letters, it sounded like she was settling in well, finding Istanbul and its people fascinating, just as she thought she would. Salih had left Istanbul at the beginning of March; going first to his family home in Anatolia where he was to meet up with the cousin who was to accompany him to Pakistan, and thereafter to Kabul if possible.

Mags wrote to Barbara and Sean, suggesting they visit her soon after Salih's departure; it would take her mind off his dangerous journey, she'd said, if she could start planning Sean's 'Introductory Tour' of the city. So on Barbara's return from Oxford, they had booked their tickets and planned to stay with Mags for two weeks at the end of March.

Ataturk Airport, late March 1996

'Good old THY, I've hardly ever known them to be delayed,' said Barbara, as they waited by the luggage carousel. Sean went off to grab a luggage trolley. Bored with gazing at the empty, stationary conveyor belt, Barbara looked over and watched him returning; this kind, good-looking man who had brought such love, support and contentment into her life.

'What're you smiling at?' he said as manoeuvred the trolley between them. Barbara took his hand and kissed him on the cheek.

'Oh, just happy, that's all. And excited. I'm dying to show you Istanbul, and it's been ages since we've seen Mags, too, of course.'

'Well *she* certainly sounded excited about it on the phone, too, didn't she? Looks like I'll have a couple of excited women on my hands for the next fortnight—Lucky me!' he winked at Barbara. The carousel lurched into life, and Sean moved forward, ready to wrestle their bags from it. Once he had loaded them onto the trolley, they made their way to the exit.

'There she is, look!' Barbara jumped up and down, waving. 'Mags! Mags! Here we are! Over HERE!'

Sean turned to Barbara: 'Who's that with her?' he asked. '*Is* he with her? The young lad there?'

'Oh goodness, that's Ali,' she said. 'Mehmet's brother. How sweet of him to come with her to meet us.' '*Merhaba canimlar! Istanbul'da hoş geldiniz!*' Mags stood with Ali, just inside the automatic doors to the airport's main exit. Behind them, through the glass, taxi drivers stood about, leaning on one another's cars; smoking; each twirling beads idly in one hand as they chatted; greeting the arrival of each driver known to them; they laughed; spat . . .

Acknowledgements

The characters in this story are fictitious, although in each there are represented numerous friends and acquaintances I have been fortunate to know in my lifetime. To each I extend my love and thanks.

Special thanks are due to Ella Preece in Turkey and Fiona McClean in France, for being my 'readers' and for their suggestions and encouragement along the way.

Thanks also to Ata Qam in Baku, Azerbaijan, Lesley Cookman, Christian Guthier, Suman Chakraborty and Roman Books, and of course, to HK and memories of Istanbul.

About the Author

Dee Fitzwilliam is a well-travelled, level-headed and slightly eccentric Humanist who began writing to commit her 'traveller's tales' to paper. Passionate by nature, she is interested in pagan and Celtic traditions, and is also an active human rights and animal protection campaigner. Besides writing, she enjoys photography, folk music, cookery, crafts, and spending time with friends—accompanied by good food and wine. Dee lives with her three Burmese cats in a Victorian cottage in Oxfordshire. *When We're Least Expecting It* is her first novel.